The Way Of The Cat

The Way Of The Cat

D. J. ENRIGHT

Illustrations by
EMMA CHICHESTER CLARK

HarperPerennial

A Division of HarperCollins*Publishers*

FIRST U.S. EDITION

Library of Congress Cataloging-in-Publication Data

Enright, D. J. (Dennis Joseph), 1920–
    The way of the cat / D. J. Enright ; illustrations by Emma Chichester Clark.
    — 1st U.S. ed.
        p.   cm.
    ISBN 0-06-016968-9 (cloth)
    1. Cats—Fiction. I. Chichester Clark, Emma. II. Title.
PR6009.N6W38 1992   92-53355
823'.914—dc20

92 93 94 95 96 RRD 10 9 8 7 6 5 4 3 2 1

Dedicated respectfully to Kuching and Sunshine, and a number of other cats, and a dog or two; also, though neither a cat nor a dog, to Jamie.

Contents

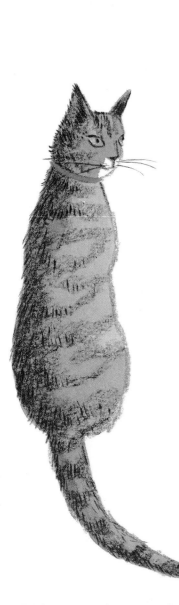

Introductions

F ACTS ARE SAID to be not only necessary but harmless as well, so we might as well begin with a few of them.

Mr and Mrs were (and indeed are) a pair of humans whose children had grown up and left home. Subsequently Mr and Mrs kept, or were kept by, a couple of cats. 'They are our children now,' Mr and Mrs would say smilingly to close friends, in the tone of voice which means: we know we sound silly, but of course we are not really, as you of course know.

Be that as it may have been, what they said wasn't completely accurate, for the cats were plainly less childish than Mr and Mrs. 'They mature slowly,' the older cat once remarked to the younger. 'One of our years is equivalent to five or six of theirs, you see.' The younger cat agreed, as was often the case. 'All that baby-talk! *We* only speak when we have something to say.' He didn't say so very much, himself.

Not that cats *talk* exactly. Their means of communication are decidedly superior, and they keep their tongues for other things. Apart from brief expressions of affection, gratitude or pleasure, they resort to sounds only in emergencies, as when their patience is wearing thin, or they have been stepped on, or are in the grip of some other elemental passion. But for our present purposes we shall suppose that they speak out loud, and moreover that they use the English language. Translating like this is bound to result in occasional perplexities and oddities and even misrepresentations. But then, absolute truth is variously reported to lie at the bottom of a well, to stand on the top of a huge hill, cragged and steep, and to reside in the clenched right hand of God. And none of these locations is easy of access.

Kuching was older than Sunshine, and Sunshine was younger than his years, but the two were good friends, if on somewhat unequal terms. Kuching instructed Sunshine, or that was his intention, while Sunshine, without intending to, entertained Kuching. The first time he laid eyes on him, the older cat was struck by the younger's pathetic air, and asked the reason for it. Sunshine, it appeared, had heard there were cat's-eyes set in the middle of the road – and he supposed they were the eyes of cats cruelly imprisoned just below the surface. Such simplicity! Kuching would have to take the youngster in paw. Since Sunshine had no fixed address, he also took him home. No difficulty there: Kuching had ways of persuading his Mr and Mrs.

Both cats were tabbies, technically speaking, though at times Kuching seemed to have doubts about Sunshine. He would gaze at him quizzically and say, 'Tab-bee or not tab-bee, that is the question.' Sunshine wondered what the answer was, but didn't like to enquire.

Concerning his name, Kuching would explain: 'I am not a Malay, nor were any of my ancestors. But it so happens that Kuching – please note the correct pronunciation, *Koo-ching* – means *cat*, and is also the name of the capital town of Sarawak. Rather pleasing that a capital town should be called *Cat*, don't you think?' In his heart of hearts he would have preferred to be known as Edward, or Charles, or even Jeoffry.

Sunshine merely meant *sunshine*. Had it been left to him, Sunshine would probably have called himself Sonny, since he supposed he must have had parents once.

The Done Things

THEY SAT THERE grooming themselves. They had been at it for the best part of fifteen minutes.

'Why do we do this?' asked Sunshine, pausing with a leg stuck in the air. 'We were clean and tidy to begin with.' And it wasn't as if he expected to meet anybody he wanted to impress.

'It's a thing we *do*, and therefore we *enjoy* doing it.' Kuching picked with his teeth at some imaginary foreign object between his claws.

'But it's pleasant too, isn't it?' Probably that was reason enough. Sunshine thought: my mother may have done this to me once, licked me all over. . . . Perhaps she did, just a little, before she ran away or whatever happened . . . or perhaps she didn't ever. . . .

'I think I may have had an unnatural mother,' he said at last.

'How original,' said Kuching in discouraging tones. He put the finishing touches to his tail and sat erect. 'If you stop to think about what you're doing, you'll never do it. And that would be a pity. Though not, it has to be said, always.' He gave Sunshine a stern look, and added: 'Do try not to swallow too much hair. You know what it does to you.'

Maybe that explained it, Sunshine mused, maybe his mother was afraid of swallowing hair. Poor abandoned Sunshine! He could see himself as a tiny kitten, unlicked, unfed, unloved. He felt as if he had a dog in his throat, or at least a frog. He coughed piteously.

'What did I tell you?' Kuching said.

Making The Point

THEY WERE LYING peacefully in a corner of the room. Mrs came up and informed them that the sun was streaming through the French windows, lovely it was, they ought to make the most of it, you never knew when you would see it again, and so forth.

'She thinks we ought to move into the sun,' said Sunshine, unnecessarily.

'So we should,' Kuching replied. 'But let's wait three or four minutes. It doesn't do to let them think you are doing what they've advised. That would be the thin end of the wedge.'

Sunshine wondered what this wedge was that had a thin edge. It sounded unpleasant. But never mind. As soon as Mrs left the room they would move into the lovely thick wedge of sunlight.

Another way of keeping them in order, Kuching explained, was to place yourself just beyond arm's reach, so that if they wanted to stroke you they needed to make a little effort. Or, when they opened a door for you, before going through it you should pause and sniff at the woodwork as if it were suddenly exuding some strange and beguiling scent, thus obliging them to *cool their heels*. You had to keep them *on their toes*. They appreciated it in the long run. A small thing, but in dealing with humans small things counted.

'Disobliging?' said Kuching, with a pretence of indignation. 'You are talking like a human being!'

Sunshine hung his head.

'The water in the birdbath – have you ever seen birds bathing in it, with little towels slung round their necks? – is tastier than the tap water in our bowl, there's a certain *body* to it. . . . Mind you, tap water can be acceptable too, depending on the circumstances and one's state of tongue at the time.'

Sunshine could only nod.

'And if one nudges a morsel of food off the plate and eats it from the carpet, it is because a trace of high-grade fluff can improve the flavour. Also – which is the *main purpose* – such actions demonstrate Independence of Character.'

Sunshine wasn't altogether convinced. He hated fluff in his food. And he didn't care for specks of feather floating in the birdbath. How they got there he couldn't imagine. They seemed to have a life of their own; or a death.

'This is exactly why from time to time one stares fixedly at Mr and Mrs when they are at table, until they reluctantly pass one a scrap of their food.' Kuching was in full flood. 'It's usually rubbish, and best left alone, but they should be induced to offer it. Similarly, one makes as if to jump fondly on their laps, then one has second thoughts – *very visibly* – and turns one's back. One has to go out – I trust you are listening – one has to go out of one's way, however inconvenient it may be, to show that one is not – I can barely entertain the idea – a *p-e-t*.'

They looked at each other, winked, and trotted into the house. Kuching located Mrs, who was painfully tapping at an ugly machine for making dirty marks on paper, ogled her briefly, and jumped up on her lap. She started, and various objects fell to the ground.

Sunshine went away to puzzle it out.

Going Away

MR AND MRS were planning to take a holiday – the first for many years. Suitcases had been brought out, and clothing sorted into neat piles. Kuching observed these preparations without betraying any interest. As thoughtless as ever, Sunshine actually settled down in one of the half-filled cases.

Kuching put him in the picture. 'You know what those boxes are for? They are for *going away* – and *leaving us.*'

Sunshine leapt out of the suitcase as if it held hot bricks.

'Which,' Kuching continued, 'would be highly inconvenient, to say the least. No doubt they intend to arrange for replacements, but these are never satisfactory. Humans need so much *breaking in.*'

The cats sulked the rest of the day, but Mr and Mrs, busy with the packing, didn't seem to notice.

'Then we shall have to play sick,' Kuching announced, more in gusto than in sorrow.

That would be boring, Sunshine reckoned – lying about in dark corners, looking miserable, pretending to be off one's food. Ah, said Kuching, there was no need to duplicate their efforts; and he proposed that they should take turns, one day he would be sick, the next day Sunshine, and on their day off they could eat heartily, patrol the premises, and carry out other duties and pleasures.

This they did, acting their parts with such convincing pathos that Mr and Mrs became thoroughly confused, cancelled their holiday at short notice, and unpacked the suitcases. They were so relieved at the speedy improvement in the cats' health that they banished any suspicions they may have entertained as unworthy. Whether unworthy of them or of the cats is open to debate.

Skinship

MR AND MRS were 'having people in', perhaps to make up for not going away.

There were too many of these people. Why did Mr and Mrs feel obliged to do this sort of thing? Too many scents, too many big feet, too much noise. Either you would be ignored or, which was worse, stared at. No doubt it would be fun to give the guests the once over, pick on those who were averse to felines, rub against them and pretend to be about to leap into their trembling arms. But it was unkind. And you shouldn't be too unkind to humans, even the ones who didn't like you. Or especially them.

So Kuching and Sunshine slipped away to Mr and Mrs's bedroom, where the bed was heaped with assorted items of apparel, some of them worth a brief exploration. Kuching soon settled on a not too lumpy wodge of something thick and warm. Sunshine was moving cautiously around, sniffing.

'I think this must be somebody's fur.'

'Yes,' said Kuching grimly. 'Probably a rabbit's.'

'Ugh! Strange, how humans change their coats so often.'

'Not often enough.'

'We don't change ours,' Sunshine remarked. At most their coats grew a little thicker, a little thinner.

'Why should we?' Though in his early days Kuching had thought it might be nice to dress up for dinner once in a while. He had rather fancied himself in a bow-tie. The foolishness of youth!

'What is their real coat like, underneath the layers?'

'Not like a *coat*, more like a chicken that's lost its feathers, or a boiled fish. Whitey grey. Sometimes brown, or else black.'

'All over?'

'I can't say I have ever investigated.'

Sunshine felt sorry for humans, having nothing on their bodies except what they put on them.

'True, they are underprivileged,' Kuching said. 'Originally, I expect, they lived in a very hot country, but they had to leave for some reason – probably they behaved badly. And ever since they've had to cover themselves up. *We* are more fortunate. Sometimes we feel rather warm – and that's nice. Sometimes we feel rather cool – and that's nice too. We can always move into the shade, or into a cosy corner. And if it rains, we are naturally waterproofed. We are tailored to our needs.'

Yes, Sunshine reflected, cats were pretty lucky on the whole. 'You might say we are the lawds of creation.'

'It never does to be complacent,' Kuching warned him. 'And don't let's settle down. We might be discovered by a cat-lover.'

Crossed Wires

THERE WAS VERY nearly a dreadful tragedy! Mrs was standing on the far side of the road, talking to a neighbour, and Sunshine, feeling sociable, trotted across to her. At that moment a car came rushing out of nowhere, and he changed to a gallop: mercifully the vehicle only brushed against him. There was quite a commotion, though, with cries of alarm, and Sunshine being examined all over, in public. Nothing was hurt, apart from his pride.

'If Mrs hadn't been standing there I would never have dreamt of it,' Sunshine complained later. 'She should have known better than to lure me, her trusting friend, across that dangerous stretch of highway!' His voice broke.

They were perfectly safe by themselves, they reckoned. They had their own code: listen to the right, listen to the left, listen again to the right, and then decide to stay where you were. It was when humans were involved that things could go wrong.

Kuching tried to explain: outdoors cats were creatures of nature, 'alert and passionate' (he rolled the words round his tongue, so to speak), relying on their wits and age-old instincts, whereas indoors they behaved in an affable, urbane fashion – if only to set humans a good example. 'On this occasion you got your signals mixed up. You were caught between two worlds, as it were.'

That didn't comfort Sunshine. 'Having to scurry just to miss a nasty vehicle!'

'Undignified, but less so than not missing it. You shouldn't really blame Mrs, you know how thoughtless humans can be.'

Sunshine hung his head. No, he shouldn't. And if he hadn't been so shaken he would have enjoyed being made a fuss of.

Body Snatchers

THE TWO RETURNED with a squirrel in tow.

'Mrs should see this,' Kuching said. 'The tail might be of some interest to her, who knows? You take it, Sunshine, your teeth are younger than mine.'

Obediently, if queasily, Sunshine got a grip on the object and dragged it carefully into the house.

Shrieks were heard. 'Take it away, you horrid cruel creature!' Then Mrs called to Mr: 'Sunshine has killed a poor squirrel! You're the man of the house; come and do something about it!'

Kuching stood by, the picture of innocence.

'Ugh!' Mr poked the corpse with a shovel. 'No cat caught this. It's been run over in the street. And quite a time ago, I'd say.'

Mrs had the grace to apologise to Sunshine, grudgingly. 'But why you should bring it to me I cannot imagine.'

'Boasting again,' Mr remarked sarcastically. 'I doubt whether you could catch a sick mouse!'

He picked up the late squirrel on the shovel and bore it away, muttering obscurely about burkes and hares.

Kuching went on looking innocent. Sunshine felt extremely ill done by.

Garden In The Sky

NEWS SPREAD OF a death in a nearby street, a cat they knew slightly. 'And he wasn't old at all,' said Sunshine sadly (for no cat is quite an island, whatever humans may think). Nothing like as old as Kuching, but Sunshine didn't mention that. 'Gone to a better place, I hope.' He himself had come from a worse one.

'Places are what you make them,' Kuching said in a brisk voice, chiefly to curb Sunshine's romantic propensities. Kuching had made a nice place for himself inside a clump of lavender.

'Our bodies are consigned to earth, or else to ash, I gather, these days. I would prefer earth, so that some bush or modest tree might grow over me – which you, no doubt, would enjoy spraying.'

Sunshine couldn't tell whether he was being reproached or not. 'Is that all?' he asked.

There was a silence. Eventually Sunshine gave what in human terms you would call a tactful cough. In fact he had been nibbling a blade of grass and a bit of it was stuck in his gullet.

'The soul,' Kuching at last spoke again, 'is another matter, or may be. Very tricky. I haven't made up my mind about souls yet.'

Sunshine nodded pensively. Nor had he. This was the first time he had heard of them.

'It may be that when you are staring at nothing, in that foolish way of yours, you are conscious, or half-conscious, of the wandering soul of some long-gone cat.'

That was high praise. Generally Sunshine wasn't allowed to be even half-conscious, least of all when staring.

'When I was a mere stripling I was fortunate enough to know a wise old Persian. Once he told me of experiments carried out in his native country. Bodies were weighed immediately before death and again immediately after. Any difference would be accounted for by the soul, or so the theory had it. First there, and then not there. A sudden loss was recorded of – I forget the details, but let's say the weight of a spoonful of milk. The old Persian did say that this might simply be due to sweating, or the absence of breath in the body . . .'

Sunshine was dubious. 'A dead mouse always seems *heavier* to me than a live one.'

'That's because you are weakened by pursuing it. In any case, we were not discussing mice. I doubt they have souls of any substance.'

Kuching went on to say that he was rather attached to his body, decrepit though it might appear to callow youth.

'I intend to stroll in this garden, and of course to recline, until I am called to some greater garden in the sky – where cats are more spiritual in their conduct, and they neither mate nor are given in mating. They probably wouldn't dream of spraying, either.' In which case, he assumed, neutered toms would have nothing to lose, and the unneutered would be in for a shock. These considerations he felt to be unseemly, and he kept them to himself. 'The possibilities are endless,' he remarked instead, 'and hence it is hardly worth beginning. Speculation is vain and quite likely to damage the health.'

Actually he hoped the life to come, if it came, would be much like the present one, plus a few enhancements – extra sun, but with an occasional brisk wind to liven things up, no motor cars, no aches in the bones, universal benignity, a slightly improved Mr and Mrs, more in the way of fresh shrimps and pheasant . . .

Sunshine looked respectful and a shade apprehensive.

Soon afterwards, exhausted by these intimations of eternal bliss, they fell asleep.

Junkie

Sunshine had been acting very strangely of late. Leaping in the air, rolling on the ground, one ear up and the other down, an idiotic expression on his face.

'You haven't had a sex change by any chance?' asked Kuching bitingly.

'Anything for a change!' Sunshine chortled.

Kuching watched carefully for the next day or two, and observed him licking a certain plant in the garden and rubbing obsessively against it. Then he knew what it was: catnip! A notorious drug. Growing for some reason among Mrs's harmless mint. He spoke severely to the young cat, making much of something incomprehensible but grim, sounding like 'morral fie-bah'.

'This practice is most unnatural. You must stop before it's too late.'

'But it makes me feel happy,' Sunshine pleaded.

'Happiness – that's all you young people think about these days! You can be perfectly happy without artificial aids. What you must do is change to something milder – this is a gradual process known as "tay-purring off".' He thought he knew what would do the trick.

Remembering his own foolhardy youth, Kuching sought out some olive stones, scattered carelessly around the dustbin; they had been there since Mr and Mrs had had people in. He took them cautiously between his teeth and placed them where Sunshine couldn't miss them. Then he waited.

Along came Sunshine, heading eagerly for the catnip. He stopped and sniffed idly at the olive stones, then sniffed again. He began to play with them, tossing them into the air, prodding them with his paw, and rolling on them.

This performance was repeated over several days. On each occasion Sunshine showed signs of intoxication, but it wore off faster and faster. Before long he lost interest in the olive stones. And he abandoned the catnip too.

Yes, Kuching told himself, it was a heavy burden of responsibility that he bore! Many a cat would have left his friend to go his own way, with what unhappy consequences no one could foretell.

To Do With Dogs

A DOG WAS lodged outside the gate, shaking with rage and yapping insanely. Oh my, the things that dog would do to them if only he could lay his teeth on them!

With luck, Sunshine told himself, he would get his silly head stuck between the bars. 'I always say, you should let sleeping dogs lie,' he observed inconsequently.

'I don't have much to do with dogs, myself, whether asleep or awake,' said Kuching coldly. 'I am surprised you should be so intimate with their habits.'

'I'm not whatever-you-said!' Sunshine felt he ought to feel affronted. 'The fact remains, we have to rub along with them as best we can in this cat-and-dog life.'

Kuching groaned inwardly. The youngster was waxing philosophical, and he had little talent in that direction. Rubbing along, indeed!

'What I also say,' Sunshine persisted, 'is that dogs delight to bark and bite.'

'And their bite is worse than their bark. Yet I wonder if that crazed creature out there realises that the gate is protecting *him* from *us*? Dogs are peculiarly prone to self-deception.'

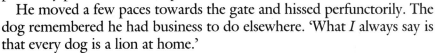

He moved a few paces towards the gate and hissed perfunctorily. The dog remembered he had business to do elsewhere. 'What *I* always say is that every dog is a lion at home.'

Sunshine decided not to pursue this line of thought. Instead he chased a butterfly briefly, leaping up and clapping his paws together.

'That must be a soul of some sort,' Kuching commented, 'since it slipped so easily out of your grasp.'

The lad was pretty agile, he reflected. And it was healthier to chase butterflies than to waste your substance being caught by female cats. Or so, at his age, he felt. At his age, he had to remember his age.

15

'I do wish you would let sleeping cats lie,' he murmured, yawning pointedly.

When Kuching roused himself he said, 'However, there is one notable exception.' He was referring to an old Labrador of his acquaintance.

'If cultivated discreetly, relations with the canine species are sometimes possible, and even profitable. The Old Labrador does much to redeem their reputation. Doggy he is, admittedly, and clumsy, and inclined to heavy breathing, and a general dampness, even smelliness, which he can't altogether help. He has told me things which suggest that dogs are less credulous than is commonly believed, and in some cases slightly more intelligent. With humans, he says, flattery will get you anywhere, and without much effort – simply lower yourself to their level and your standard of living will rise accordingly. Certainly this isn't *our* way of conducting affairs, but apparently it works. As long as you can stand the loss of self-respect involved.'

'Labrador?' said Sunshine, who wasn't very sound on the subject of self-respect. 'Must be a foreigner, then.'

'Nonsense. The name comes from "library door", because originally these dogs were to be found lying on the steps outside libraries. You can still see them there from time to time – it's inbred, I suppose.'

'But what were they doing, lying there?'

'It was all a long time ago – the story has it that they were employed as beasts of burden, to carry heavy volumes back and forth between their jaws. A game, as I told the old fellow, which isn't worth the candle.'

Playing games with candles? Sunshine gave up.

Raving In Every Alley

'I HEAR TELL,' Sunshine announced, 'that there's some sort of *entertainment*, all about us, I mean about cats. Very *popular*' – he remembered to pour scorn into the word, since decent cats never court popularity. 'It's called *Cats*, and the words were written by a poet.'

'I have to say, I rather distrust poets,' Kuching declared. 'They have a *thing* about cats –'

'What sort of a – ?'

'Of course cats are celebrated in both prose and verse, and quite rightly. I just hope that this entertainment you refer to is not meant to be *funny*.'

Kuching thought of how cats were celebrated once as witches' familiars – for yowling out loud, cats were never *familiar*! – and believed to be in league with the Devil – cats *in league*! But he thought it best not to raise the subject, inasmuch as Sunshine was given to odd fancies, like claiming to have second sight – not that his first sight was all that sharp – and drawing attention to himself by gnashing his teeth and peering fixedly into empty corners. Once it was a ghostly mouse which had vanished through a ghostly hole in the wainscot. On another occasion, so he said, he had been haunted for at least three minutes by the spirit of a large and threatening bird called Alby Truss or some such nonsense. Kuching put this down to the fact that Sunshine was an orphan, born in a storm and abandoned as soon as the weather improved.

But Sunshine had heard of some poems by one Gavin Ewart, read on the radio. Very good they were said to be, 'very good as poems', though very sad, one was about an old cat and his last visit to the vet – 'but probably it wasn't really his last . . .'

'That's the trouble with poems,' Kuching interrupted. 'They are only good *as poems*, whereas food is good in more ways than one, so is the sun, not to mention sleep. No doubt there are many poems *about* cats, but you will be hard pressed to find one *by* a cat. Indeed, I advise you to have as little as possible to do with writers as a whole; while you are looking for your supper, they are looking for a subject to write about.'

It was true that he had felt the stirrings of temptation when approached by a trim young black-and-white, introducing herself as Ms Chatto, who professed to be connected with a reputable publishing house, and was soliciting the meow-moirs of distinguished felines. Unfortunately his principles stood in the way, he apprised her, since he was of the firm opinion that cats should get on with their own lives instead of immersing themselves, not always for the purest of motives, in the biographies of others. When Ms Chatto started to babble excitedly about the attractive advances she could make and the offers he couldn't possibly refuse, he had retreated, with as much courtesy as he could summon up.

Sunshine was in a fit of loquacity for once. He went on about a postcard he had spotted while gazing idly into the newsagent's window, of a scared-looking cat and a huge creature, maybe a hippopo-something, sitting in a small, sinking boat. The huge creature, who clutched a small musical instrument, was saying: 'I have a confession to make – I'm not really an owl.' This had baffled him, until he remembered some verses about an owl and a pussy-cat going to sea in a beautiful pea-green boat. 'So you see, poetry can be useful in explaining things like pictures.'

Kuching groaned. A cat foolish enough to embark on a voyage with an owl might well be foolish enough to consort with a hippopotamus, but he had never met one daft enough to do either.

'Some of us have been famous explorers – cats have excellent sea legs, four of them in fact. But no self-respecting feline would set sail in a *pea-green* boat, which is clearly the sort of vessel that rats would desert, had they ever settled there in the first place!'

The poem in question, he continued, was sheer, unbridled fantasy: it actually alleged that the cat and the owl fell in love and planned to get married! 'A gross libel – and nothing short of paw-nography. It ought to be banned!'

Having paused to recover himself, he said, 'The sapient old Persian once told me that it was written in their holy books that poets rave – or was it *rove*? – in every alley, preaching what they never practise. It may be that what he said was *valley*, but it comes to the same thing.'

The truth was, as a small kitten Kuching had been badly frightened by a poem about a pussy in a well, and he had never quite got over it.

It had grown late. 'High time Mr and Mrs went to bed,' he said. 'Let's remind them.' This was done by herding them into the bedroom, which wasn't easy if they were being more than normally obtuse, and fixing one's gaze meaningfully on the bed.

Tending The Sick

AFTER MRS FELL down the stairs, creating a fearful racket (and also breaking a leg), she was confined to bed.

'We must go and lie on her,' Kuching declared, 'so she can't move about. Moving about is bad for broken legs, and humans have so much leg to break.'

So they did, pleasantly sunny though it was out in the fresh air. Mrs thought she would be crushed to death – cats have a gift for making themselves preternaturally heavy – but was gratified to have their company.

Mr behaved very badly, complaining that all his free time, and he didn't have much of it, went on feeding the animals and cleaning out their litter-tray. ('Did you hear that?' whispered Sunshine. 'He said he had to keep changing the litter because we used it.' 'We only use it because he changes it. If something has a purpose, it would be unkind to deny it fulfilment.' Not that they ever filled it full, Sunshine reflected. 'Otherwise,' Kuching added, 'I prefer a well-kept flowerbed.') Mr wasn't aware that Mrs Next Door was also feeding them in her kitchen, as she was afraid they might be neglected in the house of pain. So nervous was she of giving them the wrong food that she gave them hers, parts of which were novel and quite appealing. Sunshine took to mild curry, and Kuching formed a taste for cheese soufflé, followed by melon from which the seeds had been removed.

Mr fell over the vacuum cleaner, and swore. The cats reckoned it served both of them right, Mr and the vacuum cleaner. They just looked innocent and rather sad; 'pale and interesting' was how Kuching put it, though it was hard for them to look pale.

Before long Mrs was back on her feet, hobbling about the house much as usual. 'You see?' said Kuching. 'It worked. I hope she's grateful.'

Ye Shall Be As Gods

AT TIMES KUCHING had been disposed to wonder if he were not what a more than usually perceptive human once called a 'Beyond-cat': a cat of outstanding intellect.

That particular cat, Kuching informed his young friend, had taught himself to converse with humans. This was a misguided ambition, and one which he, Kuching, was above. Even so, the Beyond-cat was a witty and astute character. When he told her that a saucer of milk would be acceptable, the Mrs of the house was so amazed that she spilt most of it. She felt obliged to apologise – as if she had spilt the milk in the vicar's lap – whereupon the Beyond-cat remarked coolly, 'So what? It's not *my* Axminster.'

An Axminster, Kuching had to explain, was a kind of costly floor-covering much prized by humans. Sunshine wanted to hear the rest of the story. Surely the Beyond-cat rose to great heights in the world, and became a privy councillor, or a justice of the peace, or a dairyman, or at least a professor?

'Apparently,' Kuching said gravely, 'he was assassinated by a large ginger of strong conservative persuasions.' Which was a somewhat extreme measure, in his opinion, but not without justification. 'Once we start listening to humans there'll be no end to it. They'll insist on pouring out their sorrows without cease; they'll demand words of solace and approbation and encouragement in return. They won't be interested in us, *as such*, apart from appropriating what little of our wisdom they can grasp and then passing it off as their own. They might take it into their heads to pray to us and clamour for favours: if being treated as *gods* were all that enjoyable we would never have left Egypt!' No, he continued, let dogs – though of course they lacked the intelligence to learn human speech, for if they could, they most certainly would – let dogs bear the brunt of it. They were sick-of-antic by nature, and made sympathetic listeners, if only

21

because of the lugubrious expression on their faces. He exempted the Labrador from these strictures: the old fellow made certain concessions for the sake of a quiet life, but he knew where to stop. '*There's* a dog who may look at a king – supposing he ever wanted to.'

Visiting The Vet

THEY WERE TO go to the vet for their regular check-up. To begin with, the statutory resistance was offered: they didn't care to do what hadn't been their idea in the first place; however well one might feel, there was always a chance that the vet would shake his or her head and sigh; they didn't like baskets, and they objected to being helped in, and so on. Nobody got scratched, it should be said. And as soon as they were in their baskets, having entered head first with no more than a deferential pressure on their rears, they turned swiftly about so that they could look out.

Thereafter they rather enjoyed the trip. There were always some scruffy dogs at the vet's, far too frightened to bark, who whimpered whenever the nurse appeared, and did worse things, causing their red-faced Mr's and Mrs's to get down on their knees with dishcloths and towels. But everyone there admired the cats, the vet included (as you could tell from the affectionate way he pressed their flesh), especially when it was time to leave and, entering their baskets voluntarily now, they repeated the nimble swivelling manœuvre. The baskets were a tight fit, acquired when they were altogether smaller: how did they do it!, the gathered humans marvelled. The baskets were kept in the garage, out of sight so as not to upset them (thus Mr and Mrs reasoned), and the cats had practised on the sly when the garage door was left open. By now they were dab hands at it; they could turn through 180 degrees on a sixpence, Kuching declared.

'When you're inside a car it doesn't sound quite so noisy as when you're outside,' said Kuching. 'I doubt whether it's much safer, though.'

They were toying with something particularly tasty, the sort of little treat they were always given after what was popularly believed to be a 'traumatic experience'.

'It's nice when we're back home,' Sunshine said, licking his chops.

'Still, vets are a well-meaning, often amiable, and sometimes useful set. I have to admit that I generally feel better after a visit, though that may be purely coincidental.'

'Mr and Mrs always seem worse after they've been to see their own vet,' Sunshine commented.

'I've noticed that. They complain far more afterwards than they did before. About having to give this up, and give that up, and drinking nasty stuff out of sticky bottles. It seems that humans have to make do with an inferior class of vet. Sad, but I suppose it stands to reason.'

Sunshine And Rain

S UNSHINE HAD GONE out for his constitutional. Now it was growing dark, and he still wasn't back. It was most unusual for him to be away so long.

It had been raining hard, Kuching assured himself, and Sunshine must have sheltered somewhere, and then dozed off.

The next morning Kuching looked for him in the garden, and outside in the street. In vain. Might he have gone to the library? the Old Labrador asked. Not him, said Kuching. The dog shook his head mournfully, spattering Kuching in the process, and promised to keep a weather eye open. Kuching felt really worried, but was too proud to show it. Mrs wasn't. She scoured the neighbourhood, stopping passers-by to ask if they had seen a cat: 'a young tabby, fairly ordinary in appearance, nothing special . . .' (Sunshine wouldn't like to hear that) . . . 'but a *good* boy,' Mrs added. Thanks to me, Kuching reflected, I've done my best by him, no cat could do more.

The day wore on, and there was no sign of him.

Darkness fell again. Kuching didn't want to have gloomy thoughts, so he drew on his stock of cheery ones.

Such as:

> Boys will be boys,
> Youth's the season made for joys,

and:

> Nothing adventure, nothing gain,

and:

> O mischief mine, where are you roaming?

(he couldn't remember whether there was an answer to that), and

It's a long lane that has no turning

(there were lots of long lanes in the vicinity), and

> Mid pleasures and palaces though we may roam,
> If it isn't too humble, there's no place like home,

and:

> He wandered lonely in a cloud

(poor Sunshine!), and

> Ah! gentle, homely, timid soul,
> Friend and associate till today,
> So far removed from brimming bowl,
> No longer half so sleek and gay

(which wasn't all that cheering), and

> Worse things happen at sea

(but that wasn't saying much!), and

> Teach us to care and not to care,
> Teach us to sit still.

By this time he was thoroughly cast down. 'Least thought, soonest mended,' he tried to persuade himself, and retired dismally for the night.

Early the next morning, just as Kuching was nostalgically sniffing old scents in the garden, there came a whizzing sound accompanied by the headlong arrival of Sunshine, ears flat back, eyes popping out of his head.

Between gasps he told how he had taken shelter from the rain in a shed, and while he wasn't looking a man had come and locked the door, and he couldn't get out until much, much later, when the man came back and opened it. It was a tiny shed, full of metal things used for making holes in the earth and filling them in again; there was hardly room to swing a human. He had scratched and scratched at the door, look, his claws were worn right down. And his stomach had gone all hollow.

Then Mrs came out, gave a cry of joy, picked Sunshine up, hugged him to her bosom, and covered him in kisses. You would think she was going to eat him, though Sunshine must have been hungry enough to eat her.

It was too much for Kuching, he couldn't abide such soppiness. Wait till he got the young fellow alone! He remembered another wise saying, 'A bad penny always comes back', and stole silently away.

Good Sport

An amiable young cat had settled nearby whose name was Yorker, because he had been born up north. Unfortunately his first Mr and Mrs had turned vegetarian for moral reasons, and expected him to follow suit; before long, he was beginning to feel very unwell, so he attached himself to a family he espied through the window of a café, enthusiastically tucking into black pudding and fish and chips. They were touring the Lake District, and brought him back with them as a 'souvenir' – whatever that might be.

Yorker, it appeared, was interested in cricket, which was unusual since cats are not notably sporty, except in their own unpremeditated fashion.

Cricket, Kuching wondered idly, was it like tennis?

Tennis, he had heard a story about that, Sunshine said. There were two cats sitting on a wall, watching a game of tennis. One of them was bored. The other one followed the proceedings intently, his eyes following the ball from side to side. 'I can't think what you see in this game,' remarked the bored one. The other replied, 'Ah, but my father's in that racket!'

Kuching would have paled could he have done so. As it was, his invisible aura turned a murky off-white. 'DO YOU THINK THAT STORY IS AMUSING?' he uttered in capital letters.

Sunshine didn't know what he thought of it. He didn't understand it. 'What *is* a rack-it?' he asked timidly.

'FORGET IT!' Kuching snarled.

Yorker didn't *play* cricket. But he would settle in a corner of the school playing-field and watch the human kittens for hours on end, purring appreciatively every now and then.

'When they play that other game, with a bigger ball, foot-ball it's called,' said Sunshine, hoping to recover lost ground, 'there's a little dog who joins in. He rushes after the ball, this way and that, tripping them up.'

'Dogs do that sort of thing,' Kuching said scornfully. 'They cannot reconcile themselves to being dogs. Which is understandable.' It was not so very long ago that he used to chase a ping-pong ball; but only, he insisted, to divert Mr and Mrs when they showed signs of listlessness.

With Respect

ONCE AGAIN THEY were discussing that ever-interesting topic, human beings: an alien race and yet, they had to admit, their nearest (though not *very* near) of kin.

'They are gifted in certain ways,' Kuching allowed.

'They open tins well,' Sunshine agreed.

'But they are so slow to learn.'

'I'm not,' said Sunshine proudly. 'I learnt about dogs when I was quite young, and I learnt not to bother to chase birds unless they were very young or not very fit.'

'I trust you have learnt more than that.' Kuching sounded ratty. 'I was attempting to point out that, while it would be an exaggeration to say they *never* learn, they do take so long about it. For example, Mr continues to trip over me, and not only in the dark, which could be ascribed to a genetic disability. Particularly, I have noticed, after he has been swallowing liquid from a bottle. And yet again this morning he stepped on my tail. Oh, I know he didn't *mean* to, humans are forever doing things without *meaning* to. And his apologies were profuse and earnest, if lacking in grace. But even so . . .'

Sunshine observed that humans had learnt one thing: 'to respect us.'

'More or less.' Kuching spoke with faint unease. 'But that doesn't count – it's innate.'

'In what?'

'In their nate-ture.'

A tiny fear nagged at him. Respect was all very well, but some crank might come up with the theory that cat-hood ought to be fully respected, and therefore cats should be independent and self-governing (weren't they already?), and free to lead their own authentic lives, forage for their food, be left out in all weathers to conduct themselves 'naturally', fend off predators, cure themselves with the herbs of the field, and so forth. He had a suspicion that respect could be carried too far – respect could leave you worse off than you were before.

'Give them their due – they do make pleasant company,' he said, moving away from the danger spot. 'Especially for solitary cats, and old ones, less fortunate than we are.'

Sunshine beamed. 'Yes, we have each other, but it's nice to have humans around too. I don't think I would ever want to be without one or two of them now. Somehow, a house doesn't seem complete without them.'

Wherewith the two of them went off to show Mr and Mrs a measure of unsolicited and disinterested affection.

Native Accents

S UNSHINE WAS CHATTERING with unaccustomed vivacity about a young Siamese he had met that morning, another new arrival in the neighbourhood. The neighbourhood was definitely 'going up'.

'She's – er – so *fisticated*, very – er, *svelte*, and *suave*. She was making noises, sounds I mean, that were positively *oppa-ratic*. She told me how she slept on silken cushions stuffed with top-quality human hair, and fed on goldfish and amah's milk.' Whatever amah's milk was.

Typically shameless, Kuching thought. Whatever an amah was.

'You should have seen her on top of the wall, dashing along in leaps and bounds!'

'Your vocabulary has certainly grown by leaps and bounds,' Kuching said sarcastically. He continued in tones more earnest: 'I do not wish to appear racist, or even uncharitable, and I would like to see you widening the rather narrow circle of your acquaintances. But they're fearful show-offs, that lot. You would think they were royalty. Clambering all over the place like mountaineers or goats. Cats should climb only for some pressing reason. Nor can I say *I* admire their native accents. Trying to sing, indeed! I have heard more harmonious sounds coming from the school down the road.'

'It takes all sorts,' muttered Sunshine, wounded. The Siamese had taught him some new concepts, including *concept*. And she was very pretty, as well.

Reasoning Why

'WHAT A DREADFUL screeching!' Sunshine groused. He had been about to drop off. 'That's the umpteenth time today.'

A football match at Fulham, Kuching surmised; unless a world war had broken out, of course, or an in-flew-enza.

'It's an *amble-lance*,' he stated. 'And it's for taking sick and wounded humans to the hospital. Hospital? – oh, that's a kind of vet's where you stay the night.'

'But why does it have to make so much noise? It can't be good for the sick humans. They ought to be resting in peace.'

'It makes those loud, alarming noises so that it won't run into other humans on the way and knock them down. That's why. If it did, they'd have to be put inside as well, and it would soon be too full to move, wouldn't it?'

'Oh.' Sunshine wouldn't want to be knocked down by a noisy amble-lance of all things.

'Sometimes humans do have good reasons for doing what they do.'

Sunshine didn't doubt it; only it was such a trial, trying to find out what the reasons were.

I T HAPPENED THAT Sunshine bumped (but not literally) into the young Siamese on the corner of the street, where he had been loitering just outside Kuching's field of vision.

Her name, the young lady informed him, was Sirikit. 'Not, as some vulgar persons like to joke, Sirikitty.' It was a proper Siamese name, associated with royalty.

She must have come a very long way, then? Not exactly; as a matter of fact she was born quite near, at a well-bred establishment in Richmond. 'Born in exile, you could say.'

'Ah, if only you had your rights . . .' said Sunshine feelingly.

'I do have them,' she replied cheerfully, stretching out a long, elegant leg. She seemed to be wearing brown silk stockings. Very fetching, to his way of looking.

'That's all right, then.' He felt crestfallen, his sympathy wasn't wanted. 'I mean, it's something.'

'It's a lot in my case.' She licked a charming paw. 'I make sure of that.'

'Well, if there's anything I can do, to make you feel at home, say – if that's what you want to feel . . .'

'There's nothing at the moment, thank you all the same.'

They fell into an amicable silence. Sunshine hoped he wasn't staring too obviously.

'You have nice eyes, you know,' she said.

He dropped them.

'I imagine you do have a name as well?'

He blushed, so to speak, apologised, and stammered out his name.

'Never mind.' She sounded faintly disappointed. 'I don't suppose you had any say in the matter. Maybe I shall call you Little Ray.'

He did his best to look gratified.

'Your friend is a bit of a stick-in-the-mud, isn't he? I've noticed the two of you around.'

'Well . . .' Sunshine didn't wish to run his friend down. He had heard of females coming between one male and another. 'He *is* rather set in his ways, I suppose. He's much older than me, of course. But he's a good sort, a very good sort, at bottom.' Oh, he shouldn't have said that rude word. 'Sorry,' he added.

'What for?'

'I mean, he is *fundamentally decent*, and *knowledgeable*, and *judicious*, and always ready to *advise* and *admonish*.'

'My, you do know some big words!'

Sunshine had picked them up from Kuching, who had more than once applied them to himself.

'I would have called him a *pompous wiseacre*,' Sirikit opined tunefully.

Sunshine wondered what that expression signified. He knew *wise*, of course, but . . .

'One who always knows what's best for others. And he could do with more exercise, his stomach is sagging. Look at me.' He was doing that already. 'I exercise all the time. Watch this – but don't come too near, or you might get hurt.'

She did some exercises. He supposed that that was what she was doing. He was astounded and enthralled. Struck speechless, all he could manage was an admiring squeak. It appeared to suffice.

'Ah, that did me a power of good.
And now it's mealtime!'
she yowled musically.
'See you later,
Alley-Kater!'
And she vanished.

Sunshine vowed that
he too would do extrasizes.

All Those Foreigners

K UCHING WAS SHAKING his head, metaphorically. Of late he had observed a Burmese parading ostentatiously down the street.

'I'm not against them *as such*,' he said in a solemn voice, 'but there are just *too many* of these immigrants about. What will happen to our proud British heritage?'

Sunshine hadn't the faintest notion; he couldn't recall having heard of such a thing before.

'I can remember when the nearest we had to a foreigner in these parts was a Manx. A comical sight, but inoffensive. We nicknamed him Humpty Rumpty, we were always polite to him and never mentioned his missing tail, except behind his back. We used to tell him he shouldn't sell himself short. . . . His purr was not unmelodious —'

'What happened to it?' Sunshine interrupted fearfully. 'Was it cut off?'

'The purr? Oh, the tail. They say that in the dim distant past there was a great flood, that's to say, it rained cats and — it rained very heavily for forty days, and nights as well. The cats, who had smelt it coming, built a large commodious vessel called Ark — after the arkitect who designed it — so they could sail away and find dry land. When the time came to set off, the Manx was delayed — he had been sprucing himself up — and he scurried into the vessel just as the Captain (the title is a corruption of Cat-tain) slammed the hatch, chopping off the poor fellow's tail . . .'

Other historians had it that long ago foreign soldiers fighting in the Isle of Man used to cut off cats' appendages to make plumes for their helmets, which so outraged the mother cats that they took to biting off the tails of their offspring the moment they were born. Having in mind his young friend's sensitiveness on the question of motherhood, Kuching left this tale untold.

'What were we talking about? Oh yes, these days one never knows what outlandish accent will fall on one's ears, for example —'

But he forbore to mention the Siamese, out of deference once again to Sunshine's feelings. Moreover, foreign females were . . . There was something about them – a certain he didn't know what, but it was certainly something.

'They do say,' said Sunshine, 'that variety is the spice of life.' Not that he was inclined to defend the Burmese, a high and mighty hoity-toity if ever there was one.

'Speaking for myself,' Kuching spoke, 'I see no great need for spice, whether in food or anywhere else. Good plain British cooking is good enough for me.'

'That funny stuff you have from time to time, that die-it food – it comes from America, so you said.'

'I don't consider Americans as foreigners. They are more – more a sort of nephews, to coin a phrase. A trifle loud, but sound at heart.' He hadn't ever met one, but he could imagine.

Not long after this conversation the Burmese disappeared, and was reckoned to have been snatched. Notices were hung on the railings, offering a handsome reward for information leading to his recovery.

'The penalty of pride,' Kuching pronounced. 'Discretion is the better part of value.'

'We're only common tabbies,' Sunshine offered comfortingly. 'No one's going to make off with *us*.'

Was that a welcome thought? On the whole and by and large, Kuching supposed, it was. 'The word *common* is an extremely treacherous one,' he said reprovingly, 'and not to be used without careful qualification.'

Weighty Volumes

THE NEXT TIME Sunshine saw Sirikit she was limping. Was it the exercises?

No, she had fallen from the top of a high bookcase – which wouldn't have done any damage, not to a trained athlete like her, except that the books had then fallen on top of her. 'The rotten things!'

'They do have their uses,' Sunshine ventured. 'Like propping one's weary head on or rubbing one's cheeks against.' He added quickly, 'But they must have been big, heavy books.'

'Very heavy, most of them bog-raffies, I wouldn't wonder,' she said indignantly. 'But I'll soon be as nippy as ever. They wanted me to go to the vet, but I declined firmly.'

'You did?' he gasped.

'He's quite good-looking as humans go, but a bit cheeky, the sort that take liberties if you give them half a chance. . . . Anyway, the books have been moved up into the attic, a place I steer clear of. My guess is, there are mice up there, and I should be expected to chase after them. And that's not my idea of physical training.'

'Tut, tut.' That was no job for a princess. 'If you have any trouble with mice, just let me know,' he said in manly accents.

'Thank you, kind sir – but you don't look very fit to me, you'll need to take more exercise if you're to catch mice without doing yourself an injury.'

He offered to escort her home, but she declared that, even with a limp, she could move faster than he. Feeling crushed, Sunshine decided to go and see how Kuching was keeping.

On Horses

'**W**ORSE THAN DOGS in some ways,' Kuching announced sombrely, 'much as I regret having to say so.' He sighed heavily. 'They allow humans to *ride on their backs!*'

A policeman on a horse had just gone by, and the sight intrigued Sunshine.

'Handsome creatures, if over-large,' Kuching continued. 'No, not the constabulary, the horses. Why do they condone it, I ask myself.'

'Perhaps they like it,' Sunshine offered. 'Perhaps it's – what you said once – in-nate . . .'

'That's no excuse,' said Kuching, who wasn't altogether consistent in his pronouncements, 'even if true.'

Horses were employed to pull carts and other heavy objects – who could like that? Horses were made to run races: he had glimpsed them on tee-vee. Horses' legs were thinner even than humans', so they broke easily, and were even harder to repair. Then they were shot dead – so the Old Labrador had informed him, and he'd had a lot to do with horses in his youth. Yet humans persisted in referring to horses as Noble Animals and the Support of Kings. They spent hours fussing over them, brushing and combing, trussing up their tails; they fed them on the best oats, they dressed them in blankets, they lavished endearments on them – and then sent them out to jump enormous fences and break their necks. And then – but that was enough.

Sunshine shook his head sadly. He couldn't believe that breaking one's neck was in-nate. 'Perhaps they *were* noble, once.'

'I dare say – until the day when some impudent human managed to get his legs across them. Apart from cats, I doubt there are *any* noble animals left nowadays.'

Natural

THAT EVENING THERE was an almighty storm. First the sky was light, then it was dark, then it was both.

Kuching sat on the window-sill, gazing out. He loved the thunder: it was a grand booming, quite different from the noisome noises that afflicted his ears all too often – it was *natural*.

'There's a lot of fizzicks up there,' he remarked, 'and a lot of kemiztree too.'

Sunshine couldn't make out a word of what his mentor was saying; he had retreated under the bed, never a pleasurable spot, being cluttered up with sundry long-lost articles. He was the picture of misery, but no one looked at him. He didn't mind the flashes of lightning, they could be the tee-vee; it was the thunder that terrified him, never mind how *natural*. It was like an ear-splitting voice denouncing him personally. It even took his mind off Sirikit. ('Perfect fear casteth out love,' Kuching sniggered.) He wouldn't come out until hours after the storm had passed: you couldn't trust it, it might come back suddenly. Perhaps all this had something to do with the circumstances attending his birth.

As for Mr and Mrs, they made an effort to seem casual and carry on regardless, but Kuching could tell they wanted to join Sunshine under the bed. He hoped they would pull themselves together in time to prepare a light supper.

S UNSHINE WORE A dazed expression, so Kuching knew where he had
been.

'And what new marvels has the Ranee of Richmond been regaling you
with?'

Sunshine jumped noticeably. Sirikit had been speaking, rather liber-
atedly, about the uncouth habits of cats, especially male ones, and how
they uprooted pretty flowers and were consequently abused by equally
uncouth gardeners. She – she revealed – made use of the human fassilities
– 'Pardon?' said Sunshine – which was quite simple once you got the hang
of it. The part she hadn't yet mastered was flushing the toy-let afterwards,
but then humans could do that for her. She had astonished her Mr once,
when he happened to be there staring into a mirror and scraping his chin,
so much so that he cut his face, and said a bad word.

'But I don't think *you* should try it: one needs to be something of an
athlete, with perfect balance. Otherwise – plop! and you've had it.' She
tittered. 'A watery grave!'

Sunshine considered it best not to relate these feats – which were bound
to strike the British mind as an indecorous subject of conversation – and
merely reported Sirikit's habit of drinking water out of vases, dipping her
head between the flowers, so that they set off her beauty. Some care was
required, for while humans loved to watch the performance, they grew
agitated if the vase toppled over.

'One day that young madam will be worse than agitated, when a
bumble-bee blunders up her nose,' Kuching remarked, with the coarse-
ness which occasionally got the better of him. 'You never know where
those flowers have been.'

But Sunshine was dreaming of a small triangular face with vivid blue
almond-shaped eyes and sharp sightly ears, surrounded by proud chry-
santhemums. Herself a fairer flower.

Something was worrying him, though. 'Do you know who *Jim* is?' he asked, for Kuching knew practically everybody. Sirikit had mentioned that she was going to Jim to improve her muscle tone: the word 'muscle', she explained, really meant 'little mouse', but this was only one of those silly jokes humans were so dotty about.

'Jim? Haven't the faintest. You know how it is – some Tom, or Dick, or Harry, I dare say.' Noticing how dismayed his friend suddenly looked, he relented. 'I believe it's the place humans go to, to punish themselves by lifting heavy weights and hanging from ropes. They call it keep-fitting.'

'Ah!' Sunshine was hugely relieved.

No New Thing

'THEY ARE DRIVEN by passion,' Kuching remarked, apropos of nothing, but turning his head briefly towards Mr and Mrs's car, which was making unpleasant coughing noises. 'Also by petrol, which smells bad. . . . Whereas for us it's enough to remove quietly from one resting-place to another – from under the hydrangeas to under the holly, from the bench to the bed. For us, *being* is more important than *doing*. My self to me a kingdom is.'

Is what? Sunshine nodded thoughtfully. He hadn't a thought in his head at the moment.

'They are always carrying on about how a man's reach should exceed his grasp, or perhaps the other way round. Always searching for something *new*, forever striding onwards, never satisfied. We are content with the old and well tried . . .'

Sunshine nodded thoughtfully again. Maybe in a while he would have a thought.

'I suppose you might describe us as *sybarites*. Up to a point, of course. Nothing in excess.'

'Ah, sybarite – isn't that the same as catamite?' Sunshine put in with modest pride. He had had a thought.

'No, it is *not*. Possibly well-meant loyalty to our species has led you astray. Really, I don't know where you pick up these concepts, which you then fail utterly to grasp.'

Sunshine had picked this one up from Sirikit. She was rich in such things, it may have been due to her aristocratic connections.

'*Catamite* has nothing to do with *cats*,' Kuching added, turning away with a long-suffering air. 'It denotes *cup-bearer*, which cats never are. I suggest you erase the word from your vocabulary.'

The conversation was taken up several hours later, by which time Kuching had stopped suffering.

'Cats,' he stated magisterially, 'show less than they know. Dogs show more, excepting the Old Labrador, who shows just as much as he knows.'

'Wasn't it humans we were talking about?'

'If you insist. . . . Humans labour under the Burden of the Past – or what they call Experience. Whenever they do anything, they are conscious of all the other times they have done it. Which takes the pleasure out of it. Now *you*' – he turned a severe look on Sunshine – 'when you tuck into your food, do you compare it with all the other meals you have eaten? No. When you settle for the thousandth time on the mat, does your mind dwell on the other nine hundred and ninety-nine? No. Do you not find the delights of our garden, circumscribed though it is, ever fresh, ever renewed, and is there not a special providence in the fall of a – a leaf?'

'No,' said Sunshine obediently. 'I mean yes.'

'Exactly. For us, everything is new, however old: our senses are not jaded. In humans this condition lasts only a few years, called by them In-Fancy. Very soon that Fancy is lost, it yields to a Pale Cast of Thought. Thought is fatal to pleasure (unless thinking gives you a pleasure of its own, as is often the case with me). You won't find *us* lying awake and weeping for our sins, not one of us is biddable or unduly industrious over the whole earth.'

Whatever his reservations on the subject of poetry, Kuching quoted it quite frequently, or misquoted it. He wasn't entirely happy about not weeping for one's sins. It could be a mark of distinction to do so. In moderation.

'Humans are continually comparing everything with something else, and comparisons are odourless. *We* live in the present, the proper place for it; they live in memory, in remembrance of things past, so for them there is no new thing under the sun.'

'Oh, I don't know,' Sunshine interjected. 'I have some memories . . .' He shuddered.

'Of course, of course.' Kuching admitted genially. 'We all have. We remember that the streets are full of big, brutish, noisy, smelly things that can hurt us. We are aware that dogs are sometimes unbridled. We remember – though I can't say *I* do – how food has been snatched out of our mouths. Such memories are necessary for our own well-being. But' – a glint came into his eyes – 'when you are in the company of the Princess of the Pagodas you don't keep thinking of a certain slinky, black, green-eyed damsel of yesteryear, do you?'

Sunshine didn't. 'You have a good memory and no mistake.' He had been barely more than a kitten then, it was merely puppy love; they had only played with balls of wool. Why, they were like twinned lambs bleating at each other! (Where did that silly notion come from?) 'For you the Burden of the Past appears to be *me*!'

'It's your future I worry about,' said Kuching reproachfully.

Then they went inside to engage Mr and Mrs for a brief session of well-earned patting and stroking and tickling.

A FRIEND OF Mrs had brought her two cats to stay for the day, while the ladies went into town to visit an exhibition of someone or something called Picasso and have lunch at a restaurant they had read about in the paper. Both Mrs's were sure the four cats would get along like a house on fire.

Formal introductions were made: one of the visitors was Tristram, the other Isolde. They were said to be brother and sister. Both of them, their Mrs let drop proudly, had won prizes at cat shows. (Kuching hissed inwardly. Oh good, they had four legs, one head, and one tail apiece; presumably there were finer points that eluded him.) The cats stared disdainfully at one another, or else looked away pointedly. Sunshine tried to make polite conversation; Kuching contemplated the strangers with ill-concealed suspicion.

'Who's for a bout of clawicuffs?" he proposed coarsely, as soon as the two Mrs's had departed. 'A little flying of fur?'

Isolde drew close to Tristram, whose ears flattened.

'He doesn't mean it,' Sunshine hurried to assure them. 'He's actually very fond of a little company.'

'I don't suppose you'll be staying long, will you?' Kuching asked in a hearty voice.

Tristram and Isolde indicated that they hoped not.

'Your food,' Kuching went on, 'is in that shoddy pink plastic bowl, so don't get confused and make a false step.'

'He doesn't really mean it,' mumbled Sunshine, less certainly.

After they had partaken, the atmosphere warmed slightly.

'Do help yourselves to our excellent water,' Kuching invited.

The visitors were not so prim and proper as they had seemed. Tristram volunteered that he couldn't stand Picasso: there were some of the man's pictures on their walls, too high for him to get at, lucky for them. Isolde declared that she adored Mozart, though; and Kuching congratulated her on her taste: 'If we composed music, I say *if*, it would be not unlike his.' Isolde then obliged with an aria, which Kuching endured with unwonted patience.

As soon as he decently could, he cut in with an anecdote which he swore was true. In a town called Aldeburgh, where they were always having concerts, there was a lady who took in visiting musicians as guests. On one occasion it was a violinist, and while he was practising in his room the cat of the house entered, leapt on the bed, and peed copiously. The lady apologised abjectly, and changed the bedclothes. She just couldn't understand, the cat had never done anything like that before, it must have been a little bladder upset.

But the same thing happened again, when another violinist was staying in the house. So when the third violinist arrived, she warned him to close his door before starting to play. This he did. There came a knocking at the door, and he opened it, supposing it was the lady bearing a tray of tea and biscuits or a glass of sherry. In stalked the cat, wearing an expression of intense displeasure, and jumped on the bed and did it again, at length. After this the lady hung a notice in her front window: 'No Violinists

Please – Pianists and Percussionists Welcome'.

'A certain Barred of Avon alleged that some men went mad if they beheld a cat – of course they must have been potty to start with,' Kuching concluded. 'And others couldn't contain their urine when they heard the sound of bagpipes. . . . Interesting, isn't it?'

Sunshine thought it rude. Tristram laughed his head off. Isolde looked pained.

Sunshine and Tristram amused themselves fitfully with a cotton reel; they played tipcat; they tried to make a cat's cradle. Kuching delivered a lecture on Weather And How Essential It Is. They all agreed that congestion on the roads had gone from bad to worse and something ought to be done about speeding. They exchanged notes on their Mr's and Mrs's, with no more than the usual boasting. And on their given names.

'Tristram,' said Tristram, 'signifies *sad* – I'm not sad in the least!'

'Sunshine means – ,' Sunshine began, and couldn't think how to go on. Kuching came to the rescue with a brief discourse on the Malay language. Then Isolde explained that her name wasn't foreign, as people assumed, it was Welsh, and it meant 'fair of aspect'.

'A rose by any other appellation,' Kuching said fruitily.

The hosts led the guests through the kitchen window and showed them round the garden, where Isolde admired the roses and Kuching commended the flowerbeds, while the two youths inspected some old birds' nests.

'Just asking for squatters,' Tristram remarked hopefully. Sunshine kept an eye on the street, in case Sirikit should come by. 'Like that, is it?' said Tristram, with a knowing grin. Sunshine grinned knowingly back, tom to tom. He was enjoying himself.

Then they all took a nap. And so the hours passed until the two Mrs's returned, chattering animatedly about food.

As Tristram and Isolde were leaving, Kuching said, 'It has been a pleasure to have you, you must come again – sometime.' But not, he hoped, for a year or two. An English cat's home was his castle, not a hotel.

What Is The Point?

'**Y**OU MUST RUN and tell her ladyship,' Kuching mocked. 'At long last you've caught something that moved!'

What Sunshine had caught was a daddy-long-legs. He hadn't meant to. He had meant not to. He was only trying to do exercises without being seen to. It was decidedly unpleasant. All those legs.

'It's very difficult not to catch a daddy-long-legs,' Kuching went on. 'You need to be determined and agile.' He mused for a moment. 'The poor things are sadly deficient in both instinct and brains. Their lives must be nasty and brutish, I fear. And short. In the great Hierarchy of Being they come very low down.'

'What is the point of them, then?'

'Only they could tell us, and they're obviously not going to. . . . The *point* – that's a question even we should find hard to answer with total confidence. Although I would be glad to try, were it not that I dislike long explanations. Especially in the autumn.'

'Where do Mr and Mrs come in this – er – this higher-thing of yours?'

'About halfway.'

'Only halfway?'

'Well, perhaps in the upper thirty purrcent, if you insist. They do have certain primitive instincts, not to mention a degree of intelligence, on and off; and there's not terribly much competition around.'

Kuching was in one of his ungenerous moods.

'Certainly above dogs, but I'm not sure about rats,' he added, and he went off to pursue some point of his own.

Dark Forces

'WHY ARE YOU acting so funny?' Sunshine enquired politely.
'How do you mean, *funny*?'

'The past few days you've been behaving – well, sort of odd. If I may say so.' Almost as if he were up to something. But surely he couldn't be up to it nowadays.

'Do you mean *mysterious*?'

'Perhaps I do,' said Sunshine amenably.

'I hope you do – I've been to considerable trouble to be it!'

'No, no, you be it very well . . .' Whatever it might be.

Kuching explained in the equivalent of words of one syllable that cats were held to be mysterious; they were greatly esteemed for it in some circles. Cats sensed things, they were in touch with *dark forces* ('certainly not, dark horses are completely different!'), they could predict earthquakes ('that's true, but we haven't had any round here lately'), they could see the unseen and hear the unheard. All of which was safe enough these days, witches being more acceptable in the modern world. They had ESP ('Extra-Special Perception') and PSI ('Pusses' Superior Intuition'); they went into trances ('trances are much like snoozing') and had visions. Cats were sfinks-like ('that's an important sort of cat in Egypt'). And also seraphic and subtle, so a foreign poet had written; there was something to be said for poets, as long as one said it quietly . . .

Moreover, they were keepers of time, for the Chinese used to tell the hour by peering into the eyes of a cat and observing the shape and size of the pupils.

'Ugh!' Sunshine squeaked. 'You mean – they hung us up on the wall?'

'In that case the clock would soon stop. If only you could control that overheated imagination of yours!'

Cats knew what was *going on*. Their tails were like airy-alls ('then look at the tee-vee and you'll see'), picking up miss-tick messages from The Beyond. Dogs never knew what was going on; they thumped their tails senselessly. And humans weren't much brighter, they didn't have tails at all, they were forever saying things like 'I don't know what this world is coming to'.

'We should keep this reputation alive,' Kuching said firmly. 'You never know when it might come in handy.'

'When I act like that, you tell me off.'

'That's because you look vacuous, as if you can't remember who you are and what you were going to do. You should study me, and then go away and practise.' He softened. 'Actually it's not awfully hard work, being mystic and inscrutable.'

Mr Morris Gets In The Way

A LARM AND DESPONDENCY had spread among them, or some of them. They had heard that a Mr called Desmond Morris was coming to give a lecture about them in the town hall. They were aware of his reputation: a dangerous human, who knew all about cats, or thought he did; he might even be not altogether wrong. He had written books about them, and they (the books) were highly regarded by his fellow humans. True, he was a professional admirer, but, as someone observed, professed admirers were often the worst kind.

And this was to happen on their very doorstep. The man must be stopped in his tracks!

Some of the more concerned cats met in a corner of the playing-field to discuss what could be done. Yorker suggested that a small mob of them should pretend to be about to fly at the Mr and tear him into pieces, whereupon he would cut and run. It was pointed out that Mr Morris knew too much about cats to be taken in. Then what about appointing an able-bodied member of the community to dart between his legs and incapacitate him? No, too risky, someone might get hurt. In that case, why didn't they all gather outside the town hall and raise their voices in a concert of protest, thus disrupting the meeting? No, that was too undignified, and besides someone might get hurt.

Very well, what about the black cat who was rumoured to be a vampire because of his two protruding teeth? He was nicknamed Catula, and had been seen with blood trickling down his chops. (This phenomenon the more sober citizens ascribed to self-inflicted wounds incurred while eating.) Perhaps he could appear at the town hall window and paralyse Mr Morris with fear by flapping his paws and grimacing nastily? But Catula was extremely bashful and couldn't be prevailed upon; as it happened, he mumbled, he had a dental appointment any minute now.

Sunshine wondered whether they should ask the Old Labrador to lean on the Mr: he was heavy enough to inflict temporary damage. But it didn't seem fair to involve a member of another species; as it was, some spiteful dogs were whispering that the Old Labrador was a crypto-cat-lover.

Then up rose a veteran dubbed Old Soldier (the reason was obvious: he had no visible ears) and scolded the company in bad round terms. They were ef-feet, they were lily-livered, they were unpatriotic, they weren't the cats their fathers were, and so forth. But he, Old Soldier, had a sure-fire plan in mind. They must put out what was known as a contra-act on this troublesome Mr. In other words, they should bring in a notoriously fierce tom from a neighbouring town – someone Old Soldier just happened to know of, a certain Al Catony – who would put paid to this Mr in his own way. They could leave the details to Al; it was better if they didn't know too much. Of course Al was a professional hit-a-man and would have to be remunerated. Chiefly in odd snacks – he was very fond of snacks, especially fishy ones.

This proposal met with wide approval. As a rule the cats approved of things being done so long as they were to be done by others.

There was, however, a further consideration. Al Catony would need to be 'sweetened' in advance, Old Soldier told them. And – not to put too fine a point on it – the best person to do this was young Sirikit. She wasn't present, he noted, but he was sure she would be happy to make a little sacrifice for the good of her kind.

Sunshine froze with horror.

Kuching grinned wickedly, then sat bolt upright and said very loudly: 'Stuff and nonsense! Assuming that the End does justify the Means, in this case it is plain that even if the Means exist, there will be no End.'

During the stunned silence that followed, Kuching stroked his whiskers. He then continued: 'You have all forgotten the natural and right and obvious answer – *ignore this Mr Morris*. Ignore his lecture. Ignore the town hall and all those who gather in it. *That* is the Way of the Cat.'

A hum of assent: of course, of course! Sunshine felt immensely proud of his friend, and gave him a quick lick. Old Soldier mumbled something about only trying to help. Everybody went home, very pleased with themselves.

'That lecture hasn't done any harm,' Kuching remarked later. 'Rather the reverse.'

Mr and Mrs had gone along, dutifully, to hear Mr Morris's words of wisdom. And they had come back hushed and humble, imbued with a new, enhanced respect.

'So that's what they mean when they talk of letting the cat out of the bag!' It was enough to make a cat laugh. Kuching all but laughed.

Our Hero

ALARMED BY A hideous din, Sunshine peered round the corner. There across the street was Sirikit, halfway up a tree, her fur standing on end, in as far as it could, while a small black and white dog, Jack Russell it was called, jumped up and down at the foot, yelping frenziedly.

Without pausing to consider, Sunshine flew at him, hissing as he had never hissed before, and spitting, and fluffing himself out to double his normal size. Astonished by this unnatural course of events, the dog scuttled off as fast as his little legs would take him, whining pathetically and nearly getting run over by a milk-float.

Sirikit practically tumbled into Sunshine's paws. 'Gorblimey!' she gasped, 'that was a close shave!' She remembered herself. 'Not that I was in any real danger, being much nimbler than that miserable dwarf – all wind and piss, I mean sound and fury.' She remembered herself again. 'You were ever so brave, the way you rushed at that great big ugly brute, your claws out and your teeth bared – and all to rescue little me!'

She stopped to recover her breath. 'Back home you would be made a Mom Luang on the spot, or even a Mom Rajawongse – like you say, knighted, or lorded, or MBE-d.'

More concepts, Sunshine supposed.

'It was nothing,' he mumbled. Anybody would have done the same, he would have said, anybody except him. He felt weak at the knees – he hoped it didn't show – and wanted to go and lie down for a while.

'I shan't forget my Sir Galahad,' Sirikit warbled. She smiled demurely, and ran home to tidy herself up.

When he had gathered his wits, Sunshine told himself, he would ask Kuching what a sirgallerhead was. Better than a little ray, he hoped.

Going To St Peter's

'HERE'S A RIDDLE for you.' Kuching was grinning broadly.
        Sunshine looked around but couldn't see anything.
   'It's a little puzzle, to test your intelligence. You have to find the answer. Listen carefully:

> As I was going to St Peter's
> I met a Mrs with seven Mr's.
> Each Mr had seven sacks,
> Each sack had seven cats,
> Each cat had seven kits –
> Kits, cats, sacks, Mr's,
> How many were going to St Peter's?'

Silence fell; it lasted quite a time.
   'Well?' Kuching asked. 'How many of them were going to St Peter's, then?'
   Sunshine didn't have an inkling.
   'You might try to count them on your toes.'
   Sunshine said peevishly, 'But a Mrs can't have seven Mr's – can she?'
   'That's brilliant,' Kuching sighed. 'Answer a question with another question!'
   Sunshine reckoned rid-dulls were stupid things, all noise and nonsense, like Jack Russell.
   'I don't believe you've ever been to St Peter's in your life,' he muttered, and walked off.

THEY WERE DISCUSSING cat flaps.

'Yorker likes them,' Sunshine said. 'He rushes through them at great speed, he reckons it's like bowling a fast ball at a batsman.'

'Can't say I've ever thought of myself as a ball,' Kuching observed.

'But Sirikit won't use them. She says they're demeaning, also you might get stuck half in and half out. And you never know what's on the other side till it's too late.'

Kuching had another reason for considering cat flaps a deplorable invention: they deprived humans of needed exercise. 'Everything's done by machines these days,' he grumbled. 'They'll soon lose the use of their limbs at this rate.' And there was the personal touch, so necessary to gracious living, to be borne in mind.

'Still,' said Sunshine cunningly, 'it's nice to come and go as you wish.'

'There shouldn't be any doors at all,' Kuching asserted. It was a sweeping statement, but grand sayings always were: second thoughts spoilt them. 'Doors are an obstacle to freedom of movement. no better than national front-tears.'

Sunshine started on a story he had heard somewhere. 'There was this human who had made a flap for the cats he lived with. Then the cats had kittens, so the Mr added a smaller flap for the kittens to go through, because the other one was too large for them. Wasn't that thoughtful of him!'

Kuching gave him a hard look. Was the young beggar having him on?

S UNSHINE WAS COMMUNING with himself; he was a good listener.

'If I didn't know better, I would think that was a ghost, the ghost of *me*. But I do know better. I know I am looking in a looking-glass, and that is my himage.'

Glass is a very funny thing, he told himself. Peering through the window, he thought: 'If I didn't know any better, I'd think that was Sirikit there. But of course it's only her hermage.'

In which case, why was there a second figure, looking exactly like a miniature edition of Sirikit? A copycat! Unless there was something badly wrong with his eyes.

He hurried outside. It was Sirikit in the flesh, and she was accompanied by a small, undeniably Siamese, kitten. What could it mean? Did it mean. . . ?

Sirikit noticed him standing in a daze, and came over, shepherding the kitten.

'Before you say something you'll regret,' she snapped, 'let me introduce my niece, Pat Pong.'

'I didn't know you had a sister!'

'I don't – but I have a brother, Prem, who is visiting with his family.'

'Pleased to meet you,' Sunshine said to the kitten, who regarded him with dispassionate curiosity. 'Dada,' she mewed.

'Don't worry, she thinks every tom is her dada.'

'Oh.'

'My brother is very strict; he married a pure-blooded Siamese, and he thinks I should too.'

'Oh.'

'He's an athlete like me, but stronger of course – famous as a kick-boxer.'

'Oh.'

'I was only joking,' she grinned. 'About being famous.'

'Ah.' Sunshine did his best to smile. He couldn't see any joke. And the kitten was wriggling her hindquarters, preparing to leap on him.

'Come along, Pat, this isn't the place to do your exercises. Say ta-ta to the nice gentleman.'

The two of them pranced off. He had to admit, they made a pretty theirmage.

A Small Tribute

I T WAS AN important festival of some kind, a celebration, though the cats had noticed that it made humans distinctly short-tempered. They – the cats – came in for unwonted (and generally unwanted) titbits at this time of year; turkey went on for weeks, getting staler and staler, and once Mr – curiously unsteady on his legs – offered them a stodgy concoction soaked in a sour spirituous liquid, which of course they walked away from in disgust.

Kuching and Sunshine were discussing the time of year.

'One way or another,' Kuching said, 'Xmass means *a lot* to them, though God knows what.'

God. Not quite a new concept, Sunshine reflected, but a difficult one.

'They always want it to be *white*, but more often it's grey. And they send messages to one another, with pictures on, even to people they see every day.' Kuching shook his head in bemusement.

Sunshine determined to write a poem addressed to Mr and Mrs. Of course they would never read it, but it was the intention that counted, or so they were always saying.

Here is Sunshine's poem, roughly translated:

To Mr and Mrs

This being Xmass Day
(Or maybe Xmass Week)
My wish is to convey
(Although your tongue I do not speak)
The fondness that we feel
For ye and yine.
The funny way you eat your meal
And drink not milk so much as wine
And how you totter on two long shanks

And wiggle-waggle your small head
The way you rub against our flanks
And curl up cosy on our bed –
The adoration in your eyes
Sometimes makes you look quite wise.

And so myself I sorely vex
To voice in unaccustomed verse
Upon this solemn Mass of X
What is far better put in purrs –
You make the nicest sort of pet
That we have ever met as yet

– from your friend, Cat-ullus, also known as Sunshine

Very tasteful, he thought. It had taken him an awfully long time. He had fallen asleep several times while composing it. And he had been interrupted by a purrson from Pawlock, professing to have come on business, who had got the address wrong, after which he could hardly recall what he wanted to say.

A pity Mr and Mrs would never know about it. Every poet hungers for a public, no matter how modest. And he couldn't even show it to Kuching: he would call it dog-erel, which was hurtful.

Running Away

S IRIKIT WAS ABOUT to be forced into an arranged marriage with a Siamese tom! He was reputed to be a prince, but Sirikit was of an independent nature and preferred to choose her own mate. Even, or so Sunshine thought he gathered, if he happened not to be of her class or breed.

So she had run away, and was hiding under the arches of an ancient disused railway station in the neighbourhood, where Sunshine had secretly visited her. She was very hungry, but determined not to return home, not until the male Siamese had lost patience and married somebody else.

Kuching showed little sympathy. 'They're a snooty lot, with their talk of purity of race. Let them marry their own sort and get on with it. It's well known that purity leads to insanity.'

Still, he was affected by Sunshine's distress.

'I can't take food to her,' Sunshine said miserably. 'I don't know how to. I did try to carry some in my mouth, but I accidentally swallowed it on the way.'

For that sort of menial task, Kuching pointed out, you would need a dog.

Sunshine perked up. 'Like your friend, the Old Labrador . . .'

True, Kuching allowed, entering into the spirit of the thing, the Old Labrador was used to bearing newspapers between his jaws, and heavy library books too. A bowl of food – '*your* bowl' – shouldn't be beyond his powers.

The two went to explain matters to the Labrador, who was known to have a soft spot for Sirikit.

'Why!' the old fellow said, 'I could take her my next meal. It would do me good to fast for once, I'm getting quite stout.' He chuntered on tediously about acquiring merit by such little acts of kindness, or so the Buddhists held, he wasn't himself a Buddhist, but he assumed the young lady was, so it might still apply, and merits probably meant that in one's next life one would be for ever slim and youthful and never short of breath, who could tell. . . . The Old Labrador was a thoughtful person. His name, for he did have one, was Plato, but he never used it, because people mixed it up with Pluto.

Buddhists, merits – this was all gobbledegook to Sunshine. As soon as he could get a word in, he said, 'That's too kind of you, but I'd like it to be *my* food.' For another thing, he wasn't sure that dog's food would appeal to Sirikit.

'Very well,' replied the Old Labrador regretfully, but reminding himself that missing a meal wasn't good for a person of his years. 'Then take me to your feeder.'

It worked like magic. The Old Labrador was renowned in those parts for transporting things, and didn't attract much attention. It looked as if he were carrying a begging-bowl. But Sunshine had to stay behind; his presence would have aroused suspicions.

Sirikit's gratitude knew no bounds. 'I don't know why they call you Old,' she warbled. 'I would call you the Mature Labrador.'

'Oh, it's nothing,' the Labrador told her modestly. 'For you, anything at all. Would you care for another meal this evening, perhaps?'

'Well,' she said, 'if you would be so very kind and selfless – I had better keep my strength up in these difficult times.'

'Want not, waste not – so the maxim goes,' Kuching remarked cheerfully. Several days had passed. 'Have some of mine, then,' he offered, a mite grudgingly. 'Try that bit on the edge of the bowl.'

Why was Sunshine losing weight, Mr and Mrs asked themselves, and why did his bowl have those curious tooth-marks on it?

'There's another proverb,' Kuching continued. 'He who dozes, dines.'

'I don't think that's true,' said Sunshine querulously.

'I said it was a *proverb*. I didn't say it was *true*.'

'In any case, I think I have *insomnia*.' That was one of Sirikit's queerer concepts.

But the other was asleep, or pretending to be.

Sunshine went to reconnoitre, and discovered that the male Siamese had left the district and set up house a long way off. He hurried to Sirikit to tell her the good news. She was flirting outrageously with the heavy-breathing Old Labrador. Turning to Sunshine, she smiled and said, 'My, you look more owl-like than ever!' Even more like a skeleton, he almost retorted.

A Thief In The House

'WHO STEALS MY purse steals trash,' Kuching declared darkly. 'But he that filches my good name makes me poor indeed.'

'You don't have a purse,' Sunshine objected.

'The principle is the same.'

Being suspected of doing what one had done was bad enough, but being suspected of what one hadn't was grievous in the extreme. Over the past few days food had gone missing from the kitchen, rather a lot of food. Mr said he hadn't stolen it, obviously Mrs hadn't, therefore it must be the cats. 'I smell a rat,' Mr stated. The upshot was, they were not getting as much to eat as before since it was supposed that they had eaten already.

'As if we would go to the trouble of lifting a salmon from the table prematurely when we know it will be sliced up and boned and served to us in handy portions!' Kuching said scornfully. 'This is a crisis. We must get to the bottom of it!'

They caught sight of a strange cat lurking about the house. Sunshine was sent to make discreet enquiries, and learnt that the stranger, apparently nameless, hung out on the banks that ran along the Underground tracks near the station. It was an insalubrious spot – old prams lay in the undergrowth, bits of bicycles, burnt-out saucepans, broken crates – though not unexciting if you fancied yourself as an intrepid hunter. Mice were to be found there, and seedy pigeons, and even seedier trains. Also, Sunshine was told, a colony of what Sirikit called 'drop-outs'.

The two concealed themselves behind a tree and waited. Eventually the strange cat – they code-named him Drop-out – came sneaking up, entered through the back door (considerately left open by Mrs), and made for the kitchen.

'Right,' said Kuching urgently. 'Go and fetch Yorker at once!'

Luckily Yorker was quickly located.

The kitchen door, which stood ajar, opened outwards into the dining-room. 'I want you to run at that door and shut it tight,' Kuching whispered to Yorker as they crept into the dining-room. 'Just pretend it's a cat flap. But please don't do yourself any serious harm.'

Yorker was game. He tensed himself and flew at the door, slamming it to, and not hurting himself too badly.

'Well done!' Kuching congratulated him. 'All we have to do now is wait. If we had anything to eat you'd be welcome to it. But all the food's in there.'

They waited for Mrs to return from shopping. Noises came from behind the kitchen door, some of them caused by breaking crockery. When Mrs arrived, she went straight into the kitchen; and, as they had foreseen, howls of horror arose. Drop-out shot out of the house, pursued by a broom.

The thief had eaten practically everything in sight, or dragged it across the floor, which was Mrs's fault for being gone so long. But at least Kuching and Sunshine were no longer under suspicion.

'So doors do have some advantages,' Sunshine made bold to say, 'after all.'

Is True Love Free?

SUNSHINE KNEW KUCHING would take it lightly, if not scornfully, but he had to unburden himself to somebody. It was Sirikit. She had been talking with horrid relish about Free Love, a concept which he was afraid he knew the meaning of, in general terms.

Kuching was surprisingly benign.

'You see, first she was threatened with a Forced Marriage, so now in reaction she contemplates Free Love. It's the swing of the pendulum. What? Oh, it's just a manner of speaking. What was I saying?'

'Free Love,' Sunshine reminded him dolefully. Surely love was worth paying for in one way or another? There was no such thing as a Free Lunch, Kuching had commented, when Sunshine was passing his food on to the runaway Sirikit; but perhaps there was a difference between love and lunch.

67

'This behaviour is only what you would expect from one of her age and sex. Females are prone to run to extremes. Which is called Fem-in-ism, since it is found in fems. Until they get tired of running and decide to sit still for a while.'

'Sirikit never gets tired,' Sunshine said plaintively. 'She is what they call an athlete. Or even an acro-cat.'

'Sirikit is a champion long-distance talker, if you ask me. At times she must run out of decent subjects, and then she turns to topics she knows nothing about but has picked up in the gutters which I'm shocked that she should dabble her paws in.'

'Her paws are always perfectly clean.'

'Unlike her thoughts, then. . . . But let me say this – if I were proposing to engage in free love – and strange though it may seem there is a sense in which all true love is free – I wouldn't sit around discussing the subject with you, I should be out there – practising it. But talk is commonly a substitute for action; it costs even less than free love. And Sirikit, we both know, loves talking.'

Sunshine felt mysteriously better.

'I love talking to you,' he said gratefully. 'Or listening, that is.'

A Star Is Born

THE NEXT TIME Sunshine saw Sirikit her enthusiasm had shifted ground. Now it was the Stage or the Screen. She had been chosen, she said, out of many thousands of well-bred young beauties, to star in a tee-vee programme. Not an ordinary programme, but something more important, a Commerce-shall – concerning a well-known cat food.

'Oh, that brand,' Sunshine said. 'The one that ninety-nine per cent of humans, who don't eat it, prefer to any other. . . . But how wonderful, dear Sirikit! You will become a Household Face . . .' That meant everyone would be staring at her, and she might receive tempting offers of marriage. Oh dear. 'Do you actually have to eat the food?'

'I would do anything for my Art,' she declared, head in the air. She intended, she said, to join a Syndi-cat, which would ensure that she was paid at the proper rate. 'They ain't getting *me* on the cheap!' Not that she was interested in the money for herself; her plan was that the earnings should go to an Old Humans' Home.

How noble of her, thought Sunshine. At least nobody would marry her for her money. He imagined a palace full of venerable Mr's and Mrs's, all lying on centrally heated sofas, with jugs of cream and large bowls of – not the cat food, but – well, unimaginable human delicacies like Xmass pudding and spirituous liquids. And all of them offering up their heartfelt thanks to their benefactory, or whatever the word was. It warmed his own heart. He almost wished he were an Old Human.

Samaritans

A BEDRAGGLED FEMALE cat waddled down the road. Her fur was so badly matted that it appeared to have been clumsily glued on.

'Oh dear!' Sunshine exclaimed incautiously. 'What a state you're in!'

'I'm that ashamed, I am,' was all she could say. 'I can't bear to look myself in the face, I'm that ashamed.' (Her name, not that it matters, was Berenice, though more often she was addressed as Fluffy.)

'I can believe you,' Kuching said, unsympathetically. He and Sunshine looked her over, but didn't really feel that tidying her up was a job for them. She was particularly unkempt around the hindquarters, which hadn't been attended to for ages. 'I don't know the lady,' Sunshine whimpered. 'It wouldn't be decent!' They weren't *dogs*.

Sirikit came over, took one look, recoiled, and mentioned a pressing engagement.

'Must try to help those in need,' Sunshine mumbled without much conviction.

'Knickers! You're wasting your time,' she hissed. 'Sir Galahad!'

Fluffy should make greater efforts, she wasn't old or disabled, Kuching told her, and also *make representations* to her Mrs or Mr, who were clearly neglecting their responsibilities.

Just then the Old Labrador happened to come past, puffing and panting. 'Tut, tut,' he wheezed. He wobbled home as fast as he could and fetched an iron comb. Holding it between his jaws, he combed away at Fluffy, vigorously though not always accurately, holding her steady with his front feet.

'Ow, ow!' squeaked the ungrateful cat. 'You're hurting me, you are!'

A passing human ran over to them, shouting 'Get away, you brute!' (Or something to that effect.) 'Leave that poor innocent creature alone! I shall call for the municipal dog-catcher!' Deeply affronted, the Old Labrador dropped the comb, thoughtfully picked it up again, and departed with what dignity he could muster.

'And I shall phone the RSPCA this minute!' the human added. Whereupon Fluffy left hurriedly. 'Trying to help your little friend, eh?' the human said to Kuching and Sunshine in kindly tones. Neither were they especially eager to meet the RSPCA, admirable though that body was.

'Yes,' remarked Kuching when they were back home, 'helping others is a risky indulgence. *Seeming* to help is generally safer.'

Getting The Bird

A BLACKBIRD DARTED past, a worm dangling from its beak.
'Winsome little creatures, birds,' said Kuching, who was in one of his rare sentimental moods. 'They sing madrigals, I am told.'

Sunshine made a mental note of the expression. Mad regals: sung by birds.

'Thoughtful of them, learning to fly, and leaving firmer terra to us. A great pity they don't observe the rule more rigorously.'

'Perhaps they would, if worms flew.' Sunshine's facetious intrusion went unheeded.

A sorrowful look came over Kuching's face, and he lowered his head. 'Once, when I was a green youth, I was – to some extent – responsible for the demise of one of them. I make no excuses. I happened to yawn, and an incompetent young bird fell plump into my mouth. The shock was such that I closed my mouth instinctively. I have regretted the incident ever since. Indeed, I regretted it right away – my mouth was full of feathers and small bones. . . .' He drew himself up. 'But it is vain to repine. What's done is done. The little bird might well have grown up to be unhappy. . . . And no doubt its tummy was crammed with innocent worms and grubs.'

'It would be nice to fly,' Sunshine uttered under his breath, but not quietly enough to escape Kuching's notice. 'I wish I could fly, just once.' How impressed Sirikit would be as he soared overhead, flapping his tail! That would show how right she was when she called him 'different'. Or was it 'diffident' she had said?

'Bird thou never wert. Nor will be.' Kuching ended the conversation abruptly. He had recalled an old dream in which he turned into a bird of some sort, and was chased by huge cats, more like pumas, and he couldn't get his wings to work properly. When he woke up, he was shaking all over.

Delinquent

R ATHER LATE IN the day, the Old Labrador pottered off to find Jack Russell, and, having collected his breath, scolded him for harassing an unoffending and defenceless female cat. It was the kind of thing that gave dogs a bad name.

Defenceless? As the young terrier saw it, he'd been fitted up; that puss had had a bully-boy protector lurking round the corner.

Why, the Old Labrador asked, did he chase cats?

'Like it's what dogs do, innit?'

'Who said so?'

'Search me!'

The Old Labrador flinched.

'It's not a law of nature.' There must have been a time – he felt sure there must – when cats and dogs frisked together, along with goats and leopards and elephants. . . . '*I* don't chase cats.'

'But you're old, Father Labrador,' said the cheeky pup. 'I only chase them if they run away, and if they run away it shows they're up to something dodgy, don' it?' Not that he ever troubled himself over which came first, the running away or the running after. 'An' I need me exercise, know what I mean?'

'I believe there's an association not far from here where they pursue stuffed hares,' the Labrador said. 'I suggest you apply for membership.'

Would you believe it? Old Lavatory Door must have lost his marbles, thought Jack the Lad. He shrugged his shoulders. It was a waste of time, arguing with geriatrics. 'Seems to me cats *enjoy* being chased, they'd die out if they wasn't. But OK, Dad, just give me the tip, like, and I'll lay off your pertikler buddies.'

Seeing that the tubby old fellow was having difficulty in speaking, he gave a casual wag of the tail and trotted off to find some small unsponsored feline to chivvy. His reputation was in need of repair.

On The Box

'AND WHEN IS young glamour-puss appearing?'
'Any time now,' said Sunshine. 'The programme is repeated over and over again, she told me. Other programmes have to wait for years, but hers comes on five or six times every day!'

'So!' Kuching was in a jovial mood. 'Of course you've grown up with tee-vee, but I remember when it was brand-new, and people thought it sent out rays that were injurious to the health.' (They may have been right.) 'I used to watch nature programmes, until it became plain that they were wholly unnatural . . .'

Sunshine didn't bother to recount how he would stick his nose against the screen when there were birds fluttering and squawking away, and even went behind the set to look for them. He grew so disillusioned that once he turned his rear towards the back of the set and was just about to spray it when Mr and Mrs rushed up, making noises of horror, and dragged him away. Of course, they were afraid he would electrifry himself.

The two of them sat there. Nothing happened. In fact the set was tuned to BBC1.

'Those two seem fascinated by the telly tonight,' Mr remarked to Mrs. 'Perhaps they could contribute towards the licence fee.'

'It's a nasty night out,' Mrs said.

Sunshine concentrated his will power.

Mrs noticed that an item about the use of animals in laboratory experiments was beginning, and switched tactfully to ITV.

'Funny,' she said a little later, 'they've never shown the slightest interest in ads for cat food before . . .'

Ah, there was Sirikit, making one of her daring leaps and landing on a tin of the product, high up on a shelf. The tin trembled for a moment, and so did Sunshine. That was all. Other cats did other things, like emerging from boxes or scampering along walls and sidling through windows. Anybody could do that. Some of them were shown eating the stuff, but it may have been an optical illusion. Sirikit made an effort to look thrilled, but her nose was in the air, you could tell.

Suddenly it was all over.

'What does *tee-vee* stand for?' Sunshine asked, feeling foolish.

'Practically anything. . . . But to answer your question – either Trivial Vistas or else Tremendous Violence, depending.'

'Oh. Where does Sirikit come?'

'Somewhere in between.'

Kuching yawned, and slid away. Sunshine sat stock-still waiting for the next performance. But Mr had done something to the set, and now it was all bang-banging and shouting and cars squealing round street corners. No place for a cat.

Afterwards Sunshine decided he didn't enjoy the thought that other cats, lots of them, had been gawping at Sirikit.

Not many cats watched tee-vee, Kuching told him, only a few besotted ones. There was more to fear from unscrupulous humans, who might cast covetous eyes on a valuable property like a Star. It was called Star-gazing, he believed. He hoped the young lady's Mr and Mrs were taking the necessary precautions.

Pied Piper

'LOOK, THERE GOES the Old Labrador. What's that in his mouth? I believe he's smoking a pipe!'

'That won't do his bronchial tubes any good,' said Kuching, squinting between the bars of the garden gate.

The Old Labrador saw them, and crossed the street cautiously, waving the pipe to halt the traffic. He laid the pipe carefully on the ground, coughed for several minutes, and then explained that he wasn't actually smoking it – for one thing, it kept going out – but his Mr had forgotten it in the library after a disagreement with one of the staff, and he, the Labrador, was taking it home for him.

'Don't know that I ought to encourage him,' the old dog wheezed. 'But ours not to reason whether. A man's pipe should be in his own hands. . . . Now don't say anything funny or exciting, or I might bite right through it.' He picked up the pipe between his teeth.

'He's always helping lame humans over stiles,' Kuching told Sunshine. Once the Old Labrador had been seen taking a woman with a white stick for a sedate walk; when asked what had happened to the dog who normally did the job, he replied: 'Oh, his eyesight's gone, poor chap. . . . I'm only standing in till someone else takes over.'

Just then Sirikit arrived. She pretended to sniff appreciatively at the pipe, and sang out, 'I can't resist a man who smokes Scent Bruno!' The Old Labrador almost dropped the pipe. Sunshine was put out; he feared he would never be more than a passive smoker.

Sirikit winked at him, and tripped along at the Labrador's heels. The spectacle caused amazement among passing humans; one of them fell off his bicycle, another rushed home, shouting for a camera.

'The Pied Piper of Wandsworth,' Kuching murmured. Another of his incomprehensible allusions. 'Why don't you join them, my boy?'

Where Can She Be?

S IRIKIT WAS MISSING! Genuinely missing, this time. Sunshine looked everywhere for her. So did the Old Labrador; he even waddled into the local library, causing a disturbance by sniffing between the shelves and under the chief librarian's chair. Sunshine was distraught; he feared she was mortally wounded because the tee-vee people hadn't renewed her contract, on the grounds (they said) that unfortunately she didn't give the impression of ever having eaten out of a tin.

The other cats didn't bother themselves much; they were, as has been noted, individualists, though a female of a certain age was heard to say, obscurely but meanly, 'Cat will after kind'. Kuching was sympathetic, in his detached way. 'She's something of a roamer, but roamers are generally homers, too. In the long run.' He gave Sunshine a pointed look.

At last the word passed round that Sirikit had been spotted half a mile away. Sunshine rushed to meet her. She was limping, her fur wasn't as neat as usual, and she looked slimmer than ever.

Sunshine gazed into her eyes and gave her a tiny lick on the cheek.

'Phew!' she gasped. 'What a trek!'

There was a big box on wheels near her house, she told him. It looked worth exploring, there were all sorts of things inside, including a rather appealing divan, so she jumped in and nosed around. Then, without a word of warning, some rude man slammed the doors, and a moment later they were moving. And they went on moving for hours and hours, or days and days. When at last they stopped, somebody opened the doors and she sprang out and darted away. 'The man was so surprised that he fell over backwards!'

She could tell the way home, but it was hundreds and hundreds of miles. (It wasn't really, it was only about thirty.) No, nothing much happened on the journey back, she had been very circumspect, for there were catnappers about, and she didn't need to say what a prize she would have been. One night she had slept under a haystack, another in a deserted kennel, another in a flowerbed in a park, and then – but it struck her that perhaps not so many nights had elapsed.

'I'm dreadfully hungry,' she mewed pathetically. Sunshine at once invited her to share his repast. And so did the Old Labrador, who then hove in sight, panting as if he had run all the way there and back.

'Thank you one and all,' she said, 'but I'll go straight home and treat myself to a good wash and brush-up. You can imagine how joyful they'll be to see me, and what a meal they'll serve up!'

She limped away, not too badly.

Kuching's comment was: 'Humans have a displeasing expression – curiosity killed the cat. This shows how wrong they are, again.'

The next morning Sunshine discovered Sirikit lying flat on her tummy, which was unusual for her, and looking woeful, which was also unusual.

'It's my feet,' she moaned. 'They smeared butter on my paws – it's supposed to discourage you from running away. Now I can't do my exercises, I keep slipping and sliding.'

He asked why she didn't simply lick the butter off. She couldn't stand butter, she replied, it made her feel sick. Also it made her fat.

'Then I'll lick it off,' he said. Not that he specially liked butter; but he did like Sirikit's paws.

As for the tee-vee business, Sirikit couldn't care less. In fact she had resigned, she said, because she detested all the hanging about and the back-biting that went on.

Sunshine wondered about the Old Humans' Home, but he didn't enquire.

A MOST UNFORTUNATE accident happened. While peacefully watching a game, poor Yorker was struck by a cricket ball which cut his head open. He found this so mortifying that he made out he had been wounded in a fight with three or four ruffianly toms who were pestering a lady cat.

He was taken to a vet – one he'd never seen before – who said 'Aha!' and performed a 'minor operation' on him; though some might consider it major. 'No more fighting,' the vet promised. 'No need for it now, you'll find.'

'A warning against telling unnecessary untruths,' Kuching pronounced. 'In the circumstances there's a certain Poetic Justice about it, I suppose.'

'What is *Poetic* Justice?' Sunshine enquired.

'A particularly unpleasant sort.'

Subsequently Yorker lost his figure, never talked of toms, but watched cricket even more avidly than before. Sometimes he invited young females to accompany him; they thought he had great charm but seemed abstracted. Spectator sports were best, in his judgement; he was a bit muddled in his head because of the blow, and half the time he believed his own fib. Indeed, he would never be the same again. Now and then he stuttered excitedly about demon bowlers and devil batsmen, and yowled an appeal to some unseen umpire. In more lucid moments he would say, 'Balls never strike twice in the same place.'

'That's the beginning of wisdom,' Kuching observed cheerfully. 'At least it's better than crying over spilt milk.'

Grey In The Dark

STRANGE AND PROBABLY indecorous events were unfolding in Sirikit's house. Her Mr had been observed popping into a nearby house whose Mr was out at the time. Moreover, the latter Mr had been seen visiting Sirikit's Mrs when her Mr was away at the office.

Like any other well-balanced cat, Sirikit wouldn't have paid more than the most cursory attention to these comings and goings were it not for the obtrusive secrecy which attended them. A looking to left and to right. A briefcase held in front of the face. Doors opening surreptitiously and closing swiftly. Whispering in the hallway. Tiptoeing up the stairs. Then the process repeated in reverse.

Sunshine was shocked. And also alarmed by the thought of the effect this might have on Sirikit, in whom he had to acknowledge an element of flightiness; indeed, it was part of her charm.

'They call it "spouse-swapping",' Kuching disclosed. 'You know how easily they grow bored. Always looking for something new – whether or not it's worth the effort. All humans are grey in the dark.'

It appeared that he was right. The two Mr's and Mrs's did eventually swap one another, after some long, dramatic speeches, a few tears, and a brief, final bout of handshaking, cheek-pecking, and well-wishing. Items of clothing and furniture and various knick-knacks were transported from one house to the other, the vans passing each other on the way with a wave of the hand.

Sirikit felt 'slightly disturbed', she informed Sunshine, for she wasn't devoid of the conservatism natural to her kind. But she also thought how romantic it all was, with candle-lit suppers and the like – not that she herself would insist on candles, she could see perfectly well without.

A few weeks later everything had settled down. A new Mr entered her life; the old Mr addressed a respectful nod or a few civil words to her when they passed in the street. 'I don't see very much romance around,' she told

Sunshine aggrievedly. 'Life is just the same as it was before. I can't understand what all the fuss was about.'

Sunshine felt greatly relieved.

The Burden of the Past would soon make itself felt, Kuching remarked, adding that while in general the love life of felines left something to be desired, at least they didn't make an E-motional Ep-ick out of it.

Sunshine was struck dumb, yet again, with admiration for his friend and teacher.

Love And War

I N THE MIDDLE of the night there came a fearful howling and screaming. It woke them from their dreams, and they hurried to the window.

'Sometimes I despair . . .' Kuching said sorrowfully. 'Don't agitate yourself, Sunshine! It's only that trollop Floozie, also known as the Merry Widow. Operatic, aren't they? The vet will be busy tomorrow. . . . Look, Yorker's out there, purely as an observer. Poor fellow probably thinks he's attending a cricket match.'

Lights came on in the houses around. Voices were raised in righteous anger, and windows thrown open.

'It lets the side down, it gets us all a bad name, that caterwauling. Mark my words, there'll be letters in the papers.'

'Oh, poor Yorker,' Sunshine groaned. 'Somebody's thrown a bucket of water over him! That's not *fair*.'

'All's unfair in love and war.'

Sunshine could never understand why it was you couldn't have the former without the latter.

Just then Mr appeared in his dressing-gown, rubbing his eyes and looking very cross. 'Not that I imagined either of you was involved,' he said nastily.

Knowing how guilt could be incurred merely by association, Kuching put on his most angelic expression. Sunshine turned away; he felt quite offended by Mr's uncalled-for remark.

'I'm going back to sleep, and you'd better too.' Mr wheeled round and fell over a small stool, making a hideous clatter.

'Would that one could,' sighed Kuching.

A Noble Idea

E CUMENICALISM WAS IN the air. That's to say, there had been vague talk of 'getting together'. The cats were mostly in favour, once they had grasped the idea, since they couldn't decently be against it, or not without tiresome argument. But not many of them were sure they saw the point.

However, something ought to be attempted, something modest, if only to show willing. Sunshine was elected to represent the feline community, on the grounds that he had an open mind and was absent at the time. He felt apprehensive, but proud.

A preliminary meeting was arranged, to 'test the water' and hammer out an agenda for future meetings at a higher level. This was held on neutral territory, called by humans an 'allotment', and attended by a rabbit, a toad, a tortoise, and Sunshine. The tortoise was probably there because that was where he (or she) hung out. There should have been a dog too, a young bloodhound, but he failed to turn up, claiming later that he couldn't find the venue.

Night fell as the delegates took their places in a circle. The proceedings opened with a lengthy silence, which Sunshine supposed was a form of ecumenical communion. At last the rabbit, a large buck of fierce demeanour, demonstrated how he could twist swiftly about and squirt forcefully at anyone within reach. On this occasion no one was, since the circle had widened abruptly. Sunshine intimated that cats too could squirt, but he came over shy and didn't put on half as good a show. Then the toad declared that what he could do was spit, and warned them that, while it might not reach the moon, his spittle was known to be deadly poisonous. The circle widened further. They looked uneasily at the tortoise, but it spoke not a word; it didn't seem to have a head to speak with.

By this time the delegates were too distant one from another to confer effectively. So, with hasty professions of mutual regard, they dispersed, all except the tortoise, having omitted to fix a date for the next meeting.

'A noble idea,' Kuching commented. 'Let's leave it at that.'

That same evening a lonely old woman went to the allotment; it had been worked by her husband, who had died not long before, and she felt close to him there.

As she approached, she caught sight of the animals, gathered motionless and silent under the rising moon, and stopped for a moment in the shadow of a little hut. She held her breath. What could it mean? They looked so solemn, so intent. Were they rising up at last against mankind – or planning to save it from its folly? In either case, she reflected, it was high time, and she wished them well. Somehow she was reminded of fairy stories she had heard so many years before. She tiptoed away, feeling a new, childish contentment.

The following day the woman told her neighbours of the mysterious happening she had witnessed. 'Fancy that!' they said. They thought she had imagined it, poor old thing. In an earlier age she would have been taken for a witch.

Old Siam

S IRIKIT WOULD APPRECIATE this, Sunshine told himself. He had heard Mr reading out of an ancient tome. '*The Book of the Boudoir*,' Mr remarked, 'but not what you might expect from the title. Seems to be the reminiscences of a titled lady of the last century, a certain Lady Morgan.'

'Ah!' Mrs exclaimed brightly, 'author of *The Wild Irish Girl*, 1806.'

'Is that so?' After a muffled aside on know-alls, Mr opened the book and recited from it in a wild Irish accent.

'I think you will enjoy this story,' Sunshine said. 'It's true.'

While travelling in Italy, Lady Morgan was told of a beautiful young girl who suffered from – Sunshine had forgotten what it was, a difficult word, but it meant falling down suddenly – and for whom the doctors could do nothing. Happily, Clementina had a faithful and vigilant friend, Mina the cat, who went with her everywhere and could sense in advance when she was going to have an attack. Mina would run to the girl's parents and claw at their clothes until they followed her to the spot where Clementina lay unconscious. Before long, Mina only had to cry out in a particular tone for them to understand what was happening.

'How sweet!' Sirikit purred. She was smiling.

Alas, the beautiful Clementina succumbed to the sickness before reaching her sixteenth year. Heartbroken, Mina attended her to the village churchyard. As the sexton lifted his spade to heap earth on the coffin, she made to jump into the grave, but the other mourners caught hold of her and bore her home, weeping. At least the other mourners were weeping.

On the following day and every day thereafter Mina could be seen lying for hours on her friend's grave. A few months later she was found dead there, on the green mound.

Sunshine ended, and gazed eagerly into Sirikit's face.

'Very unhealthy places, churchyards,' she said. She wasn't smiling now. 'That's why they're full of graves. . . . Oh, it's a *good story*, no doubt, just the kind that humans love to hear.'

Seeing how downcast he was, she managed a smile. 'And I liked it, too,' she added.

Then Sirikit recounted a tale about her own country.

Ages ago it happened that the King's favourite wife ('he had lots of wives, but she was his most favourite of all, and ever so beautiful') accidentally fell into the palace pool. Of course she couldn't swim ('there weren't many things she *could* do, except be a favourite'). The water wasn't deep, but her silk robes, several layers of them, were heavy and dragged her down. Though there were servants in attendance, all of them were men, and none dared touch her, for it was forbidden on pain of death. All they could do was stand there and watch their royal mistress drown. They wept, they beat their breasts, they fell on their knees and prayed, but not one stretched out a hand to help: they would suffer anyway, but banishment was preferable to beheading. The only man who might touch her was the King himself, and he was engaged elsewhere – as were the lady's maids, who had been granted permission to visit the great image of the Buddha standing outside the palace walls.

At the last moment, as the last bubble was leaving the lady's lovely lips, up bounded a cat of the court – a Siamese, needless to say – who swiftly took in the situation, crouched down at the edge of the pool, and extended a long foreleg into the water. The lady grasped it despairingly, and the servants, ceasing their lamentations, grabbed hold of the cat and pulled ('there was no objection to that'). With some effort the lady was brought to dry land, and thus the life of the King's most beautiful and favourite wife was preserved.

'What happened to the cat?' Sunshine had listened transfixed throughout.

'She limped painfully for the rest of her life – did I say she was a she? – but the King bestowed a gold collar on her and a richly enamelled silver crutch; and he honoured her with the Order of the White Elephant, Third Class, which she wore as a sash.'

Sunshine allowed that Sirikit's story was better than his, for he was very partial to happy endings. 'But what a silly law that was – forbidding the men to touch the lady!'

'It was never observed among us cats . . .', she batted her eyelids, 'if you get my meaning.'

Do Snails Have Characters?

I<small>T HAD BEEN</small> raining hard, and the snails were out in large numbers. Kuching ignored them, apart from not stepping on them. They were harmless – though Mr had something against them – much like the pebbles they resembled; most of the time you couldn't tell whether they were dead or alive. No doubt, if you went to the trouble of carrying your house around with you, you'd spend a lot of time indoors. They did move, he had seen them doing so, but in a thoroughly tedious fashion. And the slime trails they left, presumably to help them find the way back, were unsightly to say the least.

Some clever person had claimed that snails possessed quite distinct personalities – 'but life is too short to find out,' Kuching told Sunshine. 'There are matters of greater moment.'

He mentioned that a human known as Iona Opie – 'which would make a charming name for a superior lady cat, now I come to think of it' – had recorded the belief that if you placed a snail on a plate covered with flour – 'that useless white powder found in the kitchen' – it would trace the initials of your future mate.

There were plenty of obliging snails about, but Sunshine puzzled over how he could get his paws on a plate of the flowery white stuff.

'Mind you, you'd need to be exceptionally patient,' Kuching added, 'and have uncommonly sharp eyes.'

Magic

'**W**HAT IS IT *for*, that golden thing hanging from your collar?' Sunshine asked. He had one too, but it wasn't made of gold. Sirikit's story of the decorated palace cat crossed his mind.

'It's called a Ham-you-let. Because of a famous theatrical play. I think. Anyway, it's magic.'

'Is there something inside it?' He had often speculated (once or twice).

When Sirikit moved to her present address, her Mrs had taken the amulet off and changed what was inside. Sirikit had watched closely. 'It's a written charm, or *spell*,' she told Sunshine, 'so that, wherever we may be, we can always find the way home.'

And it had certainly worked when she was inadvertently removed by a removal van.

Kuching, of course, had a completely different explanation. The custom was a vestige of ancient feline lore, he asserted, called Belling the Cat. According to the fable, a bell hung round the neck would announce the impending arrival of a hungry cat, so that the mice could conveniently make themselves ready for the feast.

'Nowadays all the thing does is tinkle against one's bowl and remind one, quite superfluously, that one is eating.'

'But there's something inside it,' Sunshine said, 'written down.'

'That must be the Men-you, then,' Kuching told him, keeping a straight face.

'Is that a fact?' Sunshine didn't know what to believe.

'Cheer up,' said Kuching. 'A rather romantic vet who died young once observed that reaching after facts and reasons can be very irritating.'

The Railway Gang

THE FOUR OF them were taking their ease in the garden. It was more expedient for Tristram and Isolde to come here, according to their Mrs, than for Kuching and Sunshine to go there, since her cats were used to travelling.

Used to freeloading, Kuching reckoned. Not that he blamed the cats, indeed he had a tiny weakness for Isolde, affected though she was; it was their Mrs, who never dreamt of bringing food for them. When the two women had left on what they described as a 'shopping spray', the visitors disclosed that they were not really brother and sister, or not as far as they were aware, though they had grown up together. That was only a you-fem-ism, Tristram said, it was what their Mrs told the woman next door.

Kuching recounted the daring coup he had brought off in exposing the cat burglar, Drop-out. 'A carefully planned and perfectly executed operation,' he termed it. 'And involving the minimum of bloodshed.'

'The railway gang!' Tristram exclaimed. 'I know them – and a wild bunch they are, too!'

Sunshine couldn't believe his ears. Surely someone like Tristram wouldn't have any dealings with those criminal types?

Tristram confided that at times he grew sick of their genteel and insipid existence, and on one occasion, while Isolde was in Brighton with their Mrs for a cat show – 'More a Mrs show, I'd say!' – he had cleared off and joined the gang for a couple of days, 'for a change'. And a change it was! Still, he'd

90

enjoyed chasing the odd surviving mouse between the railway tracks and skipping aside when a train trundled up. The grub was a bit spartan, and he very nearly got into a fight with Drop-out, the toughest of the lot, but he'd found an old pram to sleep in, which was surprisingly snug.

Ah, Kuching mused complacently, there was no such thing as a totally civilised feline.

But Isolde must have been very worried, Sunshine hazarded.

'If she'd known about it,' said Tristram. 'But she didn't.' Isolde was clearly discomposed.

'Never mind, *sister*,' Tristram laughed. 'I came back, didn't I?'

Just then Sirikit walked past. Catching sight of Isolde, she stopped dead, and a singular expression came over her body. Then she relaxed – one female to three males was no great challenge – and exchanged a few casual words with Sunshine, who was too embarrassed to make sense, though he couldn't comprehend why.

'Come, my dear,' Kuching said avuncularly to Isolde, 'let's investigate the bottom of the garden – in case there are fairies there.'

'Nice one!' Tristram whispered when Sunshine returned. 'Didn't come across anything like that along the railway banks, I can tell you – though one or two of the camp followers were – er – playful . . .'

Sunshine couldn't help smirking. 'She's always appearing on the tee-vee, you know.'

Family Outing

SIRIKIT'S NEW MR had some freakish ideas. He also had two small children, who lived with his first wife but visited him from time to time. Many cats distrusted children as threats to their peace of mind or body, but Sirikit tolerated them cheerfully. Mr's children spoilt her, not that this made any difference since she was spoilt already – she was probably born spoilt. When she had had enough of their attentions, she simply gave them a look which varied between the icy and the demonic. They retreated at once.

On this particular visiting day Mr decided that the children wanted to go to the zoo, and not, as they believed, to the cinema. If monsters were what they hankered after, then they would find them there, and it would be educational into the bargain. He also decided that Sirikit should come with them: this would make it a proper family outing – the children scowled, they had too many families – and besides, Sirikit might be glad to meet other denizens of what he whimsically called the Peaceable Kingdom.

Sirikit liked travelling by private car. She would sit upright and gaze out of the window like some grand personage on tour, and when she had seen enough she curled up for a brief doze. All went well on the way to the zoo; Mr was careful to take the corners gently, and the children in the back seat confined their attentions to themselves.

When they got there they realised they hadn't brought a basket to carry Sirikit in. The children offered to stay in the car and play with her while the grown-ups trudged round the cages, but Mr wouldn't have that. They had come to visit the zoo, and visit the zoo they would. Perhaps they should just leave Sirikit in the car, with the doors locked and the windows shut? Sirikit gave a piteous wail and jumped into Mrs's arms, having first given her fair notice of the intention. Very well, Mrs would carry the dear creature, tucked safely under her coat.

They went first to look at the monkeys. Sirikit didn't think much of them: uncouth, loutish, insolent, and bearing a marked resemblance to humans. Then there were some large lumbering animals disporting themselves gracelessly in a pool of dirty water. Next, no doubt, it would be inedible fighting fish with spikes sticking out of them. She grew bored; at the best of times she didn't care to be held for long. A few wriggles and she was free, off to explore for herself, leaving behind distraught shrieks and vain exhortations.

There was a great variety of smells, not all of them worth following up. Then she saw a human in a uniform bearing down on her, cooing 'Pussy, pretty pussy', and whistling at her. That was too much. She slid down into a trench, and up again, and darted through some bars into a soothing darkness.

The smell was right, but wrong too: as if a multitude of cats were gathered together, cats who, perhaps through no fault of their own, were less than fastidious in their personal habits. Suddenly a large shape emerged from the gloom. A magnificent feline! Greatly relieved, she introduced herself, not without the trace of flirtatiousness natural to her.

After a silence, the great cat growled: 'Come to gloat, have you?' Though humility was not in her nature, it seemed advisable in the circumstances. She moderated her bearing accordingly, and asked softly what she had done to offend the gentleman, for she surely hadn't meant to. On the contrary, she was happy – and privileged – to meet at last a distinguished member of her family, one belonging of course to a senior branch, but blood was thicker than water, wasn't it? Her name was Sirikit: might she know his? My, that was a splendid name, and so long! Was there a shorter form? Well, never mind.

The tiger, for so he was, dismissed these niceties with a convulsive motion of the head. He rumbled on about how he and his like had lost their homes and their jobs, not to mention their roots, and were con-demned to live on charity, and damn cold it was, was charity. The food was boring, the company even more so, there was nothing to do or see, the humans didn't put on much of a show for them, it was ages since he had contrived to shake one by the hand. . . . He paced up and down, whipping himself into a fury. Sirikit drew herself against the wall.

His manner of speech wasn't what she would have expected; and he appeared to think she was deaf. But then, he had been brought up in the jungle, and no doubt possessed the virtues appropriate to his station in life. Also, he was much bigger than she had imagined.

She expressed her sympathy, deplored the fact that such a noble savage – er – such a majestic being should be treated so shabbily, and asked discreetly whether there was anything she could do to help.

For some reason this enraged him further. 'Your bloody lot,' he roared, or something to that effect, 'don't bloody understand a bloody thing! The sodding bored-shwa-zee want to *help* us, do they? To relieve our wretched condition? Good grief!' (His actual expression was too violent and indecent to be rendered literally here.) 'How extremely *naice* of you! Maybe you'd like to take us back with you to your comfortable homes, to live in the lap of luxury?' His voice rose. 'We haven't sunk that low! Poor we may be, but we're honest with it!'

He moved closer to her, sniffing in a disagreeable manner. 'Well, well, what a pretty little morsel you are!'

She began to feel truly frightened, and stuttered that she had only wanted to stay and talk with him for a moment.

'Oh do stay for a moment. A moment is all you'll have. And then I'll gobble you up – one crunch, one swallow. Blood *is* thicker than water – and there's more taste to it . . .'

She dodged sideways and shot out between the bars. Turning at a safe distance, she piped: 'You ought to do something about your breath – it smells bloody awful!'

A few minutes later she found the worried Mr and Mrs and the weeping children. They were overjoyed. Quite gratifying it was. 'We thought you'd returned to the wilds!' Mrs cried. 'Or been eaten up,' said Mr. Sirikit gave him a cold look.

Sitting in the car, in the lap of luxury, or at least of Mrs, she reflected that there was much to be said for human beings. Also that a living cat was better than a half-dead tiger.

It's All White!

'IT'S ALL WHITE!' Sunshine exclaimed. 'But it's not Xmass.'
'Yes, it's all white,' said Kuching lugubriously. 'And it's not Xmass, not by a long chalk.'

'Look at our footprints! They make patterns.'

'Yes.' Kuching tried to draw himself up to more than his full height.

'Perhaps if I moved about slowly over the white stuff I'd trace the initials of my future mate?'

'I wouldn't wonder.'

Sirikit danced up.

'Perhaps the young lady will do it for you.' All they needed between them was an *S*.

She was so light of foot that she hardly made any impression on the snow.

Kuching felt thoroughly miserable; he was up to his chest in it by now. This was no country for old cats.

Sunshine looked as if he were in the seventh heaven.

Seventh heaven, Kuching pondered. What would the ninth be like – cloud nine? A cosy warm one, he hoped.

'The garden was very pretty and clean and neat before we came along,' he said firmly. 'I think we should go indoors before we make more holes in it – which, incidentally, are filling up with ice.'

Sirikit agreed. 'I believe I prefer the tropics.'

Sunshine expected the tropics came later in the year. He looked forward to them.

Casualties

'THERE WAS THIS dog by the name of Fido, may well have been a Labrador, but I'm not absolutely certain of that,' the Old Labrador panted out. 'And his Mr, whom he loved dearly, had been sent abroad, where they were having one of their great wars.'

To cut a long, slow story short, Fido ran away from his home and his Mrs, who was much concerned because she knew how attached the Mr was to him, and didn't like to write and tell him about the disappearance, because he had trouble enough with the war, and letters took ages to reach him, and maybe she could find a look-alike.

Then, weeks later, the Mrs received a letter from the Mr informing her that much to his astonishment Fido had turned up there, the worse for wear but wagging his tail madly, having somehow found his way to the Port's Mouth and stowed away on a troopship, and then traversed the ravaged countryside, braving the hungry peasants who would gladly have cooked and eaten him.

'A remarkable tale,' said Kuching, as they sat companionably outside the Old Labrador's private apartment, a modest enclosure bearing the fanciful inscription, 'Kennelworth Castle'. Remarkable, but also foolish. Any reasonably fit cat could have made the same journey, but preferably in the direction of home. An Australian cat had been known to travel a thousand miles across rivers and deserts to join a grieving young Mr.

'A touching example of fidelity . . .' spluttered the Old Labrador.

No doubt the unhappy animal felt obliged to live up to his name. Kuching was pleased that his name meant 'cat' and was easy to live up to. But he felt he should show interest in his friend's anecdote, considering the labour that went into imparting it.

'So what happened next?'

'I wish you hadn't asked me that. . . . One evening later in the week Fido was out walking with his Mr behind the trenches, and a shell burst, and' – the Old Labrador hiccuped and slobbered in sorrow – 'killed the two of them on the spot. They were inseparable, according to reports . . .'

'I am truly sorry to hear that.' Kuching strove to put on a tragic face. Any cat would have known that something of the kind was bound to happen in the vicinity of a war. But possibly there was more to the story, some aspect to which the good-natured Old Labrador was blind: such as, Fido didn't get along with his Mrs, he missed his walkies, his rations were stolen, or he was consumed with a fatal craving for exotic lands.

Kuching raised a paw to brush away a non-existent tear. To his surprise and dismay, it existed.

Up A Tree

S IRIKIT WAS RILED. She had been reclining in the branches of a tall tree, enjoying the breeze and minding her own business, when she was disturbed by a tumult of humans below. They were shouting and pointing at her. It was quite embarrassing, so she closed her eyes.

Not long afterwards a large red vehicle trundled up, accompanied by men wearing funny shiny hats. 'For a moment I thought it was what they call a Brassy Band.' Then a strange spindly thing was raised – 'a sort of catwalk' – and lodged against the branch where she was resting, making it wobble. 'Naturally I climbed higher.' This appeared to amuse some of the humans who had gathered around, and annoy others. She heard someone saying, 'Isn't that typical?', which displeased her further.

'The whole tree was shaking, so finally I reached the very top of it, and there was nowhere to go except down.' On the way down she passed a man in a funny hat who was going up. He carried a net bag, as if proposing to pick fruit: 'I didn't see any fruit.' They exchanged hostile glances.

'I slithered to the ground and nipped off,' she concluded. 'Why there was so much raucous laughter I don't know. . . . Why can't they leave one in peace?'

Why on earth couldn't they? Sunshine would ask Kuching – he'd know.

But Kuching was out of temper. 'You spend too much time gossiping on the street corner when you could be doing something positive, like sleeping.' Which was what he had been doing until his young friend came in chattering about trivia like trees and funny hats.

Later, however, he had this to say: 'Humans believe that when a cat's Mr or Mrs dies, if the cat climbs *up* a tree, it means the Mr or Mrs has gone to heaven – that's a good place to go to – and if the cat climbs *down* a tree, it means the Mr or Mrs has gone to hell – that's a bad place. . . . Absurd! How can a cat climb down a tree without climbing up it first? And if the cat climbs up, then the cat is bound to climb down again! Still, I suppose it's understandable, seeing the importance humans attach to where they're going . . .'

Dreaming

IT IS NOT surprising that cats dream, considering how much time they spend sleeping and partly sleeping. Cats have a vivid inner life. As Kuching had claimed, everything that happens, happens as if for the first time; not since the early days of Adam and Eve have humans known such perpetual freshness of experience, unoppressed by the heavy weight of custom. Dreaming is a part of that vivid life.

Sirikit dreamt she was a prisoner in an opulent palace, the intended concubine of a barbaric oriental king (he put her in mind of a mangy tiger), and guarded by huge U-nooks (which meant Keepers of the Bedchamber) carrying large curved swords. When the wives and concubines gathered, they exchanged catty remarks and spat jealously at one another. Sometimes Prince Charming, bearing a certain resemblance to Sunshine, rode up on a white mouse and rescued her; sometimes not. Or else she dreamt she was playing an important role in a play about some Mr called Dick Whittington, and she couldn't remember her lines. She woke herself up squeaking.

Yorker naturally dreamt he was playing cricket for his country, usually in a far-off land known as Oztrailya. Sometimes he made hundreds of runs; at other times he was out for a duck, a real feathered one who towered over him and flapped its wings in contempt, while the spectators, mostly dogs, catcalled. In one horrid nightmare he wasn't playing for the Ashes, he *was* them.

Isolde needed her beauty sleep. In it she was transported to glamorous European capitals, where she won all the medals because her rivals had fallen into a barrel of tar. Once she found herself closeted with an older (and wiser) cat, of exquisite manners, but more often she worried over

Tristram, who had taken himself off to some dubious camp or holiday home, and she feared he would never come back.

Tristram dreamt rarely, and then of the rugged outdoor life, and of camp followers and fights. Or else of Isolde, except just once or twice when it was Sirikit.

Sunshine used to dream of his mother, always a different one, and of dark squally alleys, always the same one. Occasionally he watched Mr and Mrs climbing up a tall tree and disappearing into the sky, which left him feeling sad. But nowadays he dreamt chiefly of Sirikit, plain and straightforward dreams, whether happy or wretched, that he wouldn't dream of telling to anyone, not even, or especially not, Kuching. Otherwise he dreamt of food, either eating it or else, since for some reason it wasn't there, not.

Kuching would find himself face to face with God, in the shape of a giant bird not unlike an ostrich, whereupon Kuching pleaded that his hands were relatively clean. (Perhaps it *would* be more comfortable to lie awake and weep for one's sins, briefly?) On one occasion Sunshine appeared, wailing piteously that he had been led astray by good counsels, for where had they got him? On another, Kuching imagined he was dead, together with the Old Labrador, and they were arguing as to whether they were in heaven or in hell; they became so heated that they decided it must be hell, and in hell you needed to stay friends. The best dream was when he himself was God, an Ancient of Days with imposing white whiskers, laying down the Nine Commandments, one for each life.

We wish we could report the dreams of the Old Labrador, but he declined to reveal them. They were, he regretted, humdrum in the extreme, repetitious, and lacking in symbolic interest. Also he couldn't remember them, because of being dog-tired at the time.

Sunshine Tells A Tale

S UNSHINE FELT SO sorry for Yorker that he resolved to cheer him up with a good heartening story. But what good heartening story did he know? Then he recalled the ecumenical evening and how the assorted animals had sat peaceably in a circle, more or less.

So he said, 'There's a cheery tale, or jolly legend, which I shall narrate if you're free for a quarter of an hour or so.' Yorker indicated that he was free for as long as it took, since it was now the football season, and his head wasn't aching much. So Sunshine began.

Once upon a time, when he was King of the Animals, the lion had for many a year been advised by a faithful cat, who was his Pry Minister. In those well-governed days all the animals were friends with one another. To reward the cat for his services the lion presented him with a piece of parched-ment ('sort of paper but prettier') or certifi-cat on which were written many compliments and commendations.

The cat was delighted, and showed it at once to his great friend, the dog, who admired it very much. Later the cat asked the dog to take care of it while he, the cat, was absent on private business. The dog promised to do

102

so; he hid the parchment in a hole in a tree, and stood guard over it. Then he remembered a bone he had buried in a field some distance away, and he hurried off to dig it up and make sure it was still there.

Immediately afterwards there arrived a mouse, who was a great friend of both of them. He happened to be frightfully hungry, and as he rummaged around he came upon the parchment, which he nibbled and nibbled until it was almost completely gone.

As soon as the cat returned, he asked for the parchment, which he had decided to frame and hang on the wall. Nothing remained of it but scraps and tatters, some of them dangling from the mouse's mouth. The cat fell into a fury, and declared eternal war on the dog, and the dog on the cat, and both of them on the mouse.

'And so they lived . . . ever after.' It now struck Sunshine that the story wasn't exactly ecumenical or even cheering.

Not that it mattered. Yorker's only response was: 'If they had all played cricket this wouldn't have happened.'

Paper Chase

S IRIKIT ASKED POLITELY if she could make use of the path inside their garden 'for a special purpose'. Sunshine was mystified. They would have to ask Kuching, he said. He was the landlord.

Ill at ease, Sirikit stammered something about wanting to borrow the path because it was long and straight.

'Like a Roman road. . . . But do please amplify.'

She wanted to rehearse a little theatrical act, involving no more than her niece Pat Pong and a cylinder of paper, in the hope that the tee-vee people would hire the kitten for one of their commercials.

Hadn't she had enough of that business already?

Much embarrassed, Sirikit disclosed that her brother was a traditional Siamese, accustomed to a high standard of living, for which his Mr and Mrs weren't quite able to provide. Her plan was that little Pat, whom she described as 'a natural', should bring in enough cash to set the family on their feet.

'Feel free to make use of our amenities,' Kuching said graciously. 'I shall watch the proceedings with interest.' Not much harm could be done to a garden path.

They waited for the Old Labrador to turn up with what Sirikit termed 'the properties'. There was only one of them.

'It's a toilet roll,' Kuching sniffed.

'I know,' whispered Sunshine. 'They wipe their noses on it.'

Sirikit instructed her niece that she was to inspect the roll, which the Old Labrador had deposited carefully at one end of the path, then propel it along with her nose, unwind it, and toy playfully with it. If a puppy could do it, Pat would do it better.

On the signal, the kitten dashed madly at the roll of paper, whacked it as if it were a mortal enemy, kicked it backwards into the grass, fell on it, and began to tear it savagely into shreds.

'I don't think that will do at all,' said Sirikit sadly.

Were there other ways of helping her brother and his dependants? They racked their brains in vain.

'I'm afraid there's only one answer,' Sirikit said. Prem would have to go to *stud*.

'Stud?' Sunshine supposed it was one of those remote and unhealthy places where cats went to make their fortunes.

'I'll elucidate later,' Kuching hissed. To Sirikit he said, 'Cheer up, my dear. Many a tom would envy him – even without getting paid for it.'

She made vaguely as if to blush. 'Thank you all, anyway. Come, Pat, let's go home.'

The Old Labrador had been making ineffectual attempts to clear up the mess left by the kitten. 'I'll walk you back,' he offered eagerly.

'Dada!' mewed the kitten, rubbing against his legs.

Yorker Tells Two Tales

O N THEIR NEXT meeting Yorker wanted to return the compliment with a story of his own.

'There's really no need,' Sunshine told him, afraid that the effort would be too much for Yorker's poor addled brain. 'Though I'm sure you know hundreds of exciting tales, and true ones.' He tried to think of something he had to do urgently.

But Yorker wouldn't be put off. 'It's my innings now,' he said firmly. 'Fair do's!' His story was a short one.

There was this cat, who shared a house with a human prince. She got fed up with him, he was always swanking and making speeches and ordering her about. So one day, when he had been grumbling about the food, she picked up the nearest object – it happened to be a cricket bat – and hit him over the head. Straightaway he turned into a handsome tom cat.

'Very nice!' said Sunshine, having waited a while for the story to continue. He displayed signs of gratification.

Yorker remarked that he knew another story, also about cats and humans.

'Pray don't tire yourself,' Sunshine begged him nervously.

But Yorker wouldn't be deterred. He muttered something perplexing about still being 'at the crease', folded his paws, and began.

106

There was this old woman, sitting on her old rocking-chair with an old cat on her lap, and feeling low. Then a Good Fairy appeared and told her that since she had led a blameless life and was kind to animals and helpful to her neighbours, she would be granted three wishes, and each of them would come true. The Good Fairy smiled sweetly and vanished.

The old woman didn't have much faith in this offer. But after a while she thought she might as well wish something, and she wished that her old chair were made of gold. And it turned into solid gold! So she thought a bit more, and wished that she could be a beautiful young maiden. And so she was! She thought again, carefully, and then made her last wish – that the old cat on her lap would turn into a handsome young prince. And the cat did! And then the woman remembered that long ago she had taken the cat to the vet to be seen to . . .

'Oh.' Sunshine was so embarrassed he didn't know which way to look. 'Oh dear.' Did Yorker realise what he was saying? He appeared quite unaffected by the story.

'The prince would rather have stayed a cat,' Yorker concluded cheerfully, 'and the beautiful young maiden was very bad-tempered, so he soon walked out on her, and had a happy ending.'

'Good!' Sunshine uttered with unnatural fervour. 'Very good indeed! I like that!'

Who Came First?

'WE WERE HERE *first*, weren't we?'

'Were where?' Kuching cast an ironic eye round the premises.

'Here, on this – this *whirled*. We were the *natives*, weren't we?' *Natives* was one of Sirikit's expressions, which she used when at odds with the local lumpencats.

'You mean, before the humans came along? That's hard to tell. We were certainly prominent in Egypt when the fair-Ohs were reigning, the ancient kings. They considered us sacred, as you will know if you take heed of what I say . . .'

Sunshine vaguely remembered something about how the cats left Egypt to avoid being sacred.

'There was a nice little perk attached. The rulers weren't very trustful, you see, and they gave cats their food to taste first. If the cat turned away, they believed the food was poisoned – of course it might only be that the cat had eaten already, which was just too bad for the cook.'

Mrs had often suggested that Kuching should take a job as a taster or tester. He had made it plain at an early stage that only the freshest food was good enough for him, and she still suspected him of studying the sell-by dates on the supermarket packets.

Sunshine was asking himself whether it had been such a good idea to leave Egypt. He wouldn't mind being sacred if it brought toothsome titbits with it.

'Quite possibly we did precede the humans,' said the older cat judiciously. 'But I wouldn't make too much of that. They put in a lot of hard work, and – on balance – made the world a better place for cats to live in. Credit where credit is due. Though all progress, I fear, has its drawbacks.'

One of which was having to answer awkward questions dreamt up by persistent young felines who had lost respect for their elders and forgetters.

He sighed. 'One thing is fairly sure – we shall be around after the humans have gone.' Which wouldn't be in his time, thank goodness. 'Our strength lies in the fact that we don't *gang up*. There are few committed demo-cats among us. . . . True, we are more gregarious than may appear to the uninformed eye, but we don't band together into vast armies, like they do.' He paused to explain what an army was. 'Then they let slip the dogs of war – that's how they put it, shifting the blame on to luckless canines . . .' Humans, he continued, were very prone to making wars. It had to do with Fate – or, for he could possibly be mistaken in this detail, Faith. 'That large empty building I saw you vanish into with your ladyfriend the other day –'

Sunshine twitched.

'– it's their Place of Warship. You see, to start with, humans get together and kill other humans. When they've finished, they get together and put up statues to them, and bow down to them and sing sad songs. There's one of them in that building, hanging on a cross – a nasty sight!'

Sunshine hadn't noticed it; he was glad of that.

Kuching spent the next five minutes ruminating, and tidying his front.

'They do say humans have two souls in their breasts, which can't be very comfortable. That might account for it.'

'But we have nine lives, don't we?' said Sunshine proudly.

'So the saying goes. For three we play, for three we stray, and for three we stay. But most likely we have only one soul.' If that, in some cases.

'What is war like?' Sunshine wasn't positive he wanted to know, but he supposed he'd better.

'It's – it's a bit like those games humans play, with balls, except more players take part and the balls explode when they hit you. And then huge vehicles come and run over you. Afterwards there's no food, so everybody dies. But that's enough on the subject. I do wish you hadn't brought it up.'

To show his disapproval, Kuching fell asleep.

In Custody

'HE ASKED FOR it,' the Old Labrador growled glumly. 'He's his own worst enemy.'

The young Jack Russell had been picked up in the school playground while nosing at a half-eaten ham sandwich dropped by a timorous child, and taken to the police station.

'I ain't saying nothin'!' he yapped, 'you can't make me say nothin'!'

'I wish this silly little dog would shut up!' the policeman said.

'You ain't got nothin' on me!'

'Keep quiet, can't you!' the policeman shouted. He waved a rolled-up newspaper.

'Read me me rights!' the Jack Russell howled. 'I wanna see me sollysitter!'

'I'll be glad when the bloody dog's owner collects him!' The policeman clutched his head.

As time went by Jack the Lad felt guiltier and guiltier, and more and more scared. The glaring policeman had such big boots. Everybody was so brisk and grim. Shouts and screams came from the cells.

When at last his master turned up, he made himself as abject as possible and crawled towards him, whining miserably, fawningly, hopefully. His master kicked him in the nose, and he yelped happily.

'Not that he'd done anything to speak of,' the Old Labrador groaned. 'He just acted as if he had. . . . It's the times we live in.'

'Where is he now?' asked Kuching. Only for the sake of politeness, since he didn't care in the least.

'Under house arrest, serving a Suspended Sentence.'

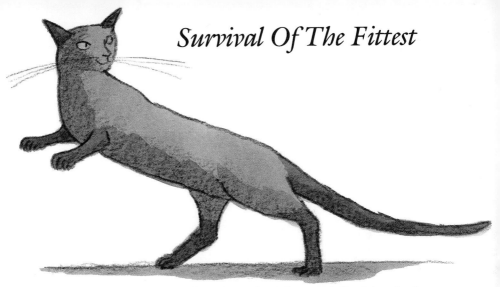

'FURTHER TO WHAT I was saying the other day . . .' Kuching had reluctantly persuaded himself that he owed this *further* either to Sunshine or to himself or to the feline species. 'I cannot call it history, or herstory, or mystory, or yourstory, because it was all an extremely long time ago. So I shall call it theirstory, although it is also part of ourstory . . .'

Sunshine was so confused by this preamble that he thought of pleading a sudden indisposition and retiring.

'That bit,' said the master, perceiving his protégé's shifty expression, 'was rather complicated, but the rest will be fairly straightforward . . .'

Their distant ancestors, he resumed, had long hind legs and short forelegs, and therefore they walked on their hind legs. 'Just as humans do today: in a sense you could say that we have descended – or ascended – from them.' Walking on two legs was bothersome: no species could rise if it kept falling down. So the proto-cats developed legs that were roughly equal in length, back and front, and began to diverge from the human species. 'This was a great step forward, known as "quadrupedalism".'

At that stage cats had bigger jaws than now, in order to hunt wolves ('which is what dogs were then') and eat them, and smaller brains ('so that they wouldn't think too much and interfere with Ee-volution'). They were known to scientists as *Felix habilis*, which meant 'Happy Able Cat'.

Later – 'this didn't happen overnight, you understand' – they advanced still further, so that their jaws grew smaller ('and more tasteful') and their brains larger. Then they became *Felix sapiens sapiens*, or 'Happy and Doubly Wise Cat'.

'Which brings us to us,' Kuching drew to a satisfying close. He had kept the account simple and short, he said, so as not to strain his listener's medium-sized brain.

'But I wonder,' he added, 'whether happiness really goes with all that wisdom . . .'

'It seems that Ee-volution is still going on here and there,' Kuching announced later on the same day. 'I've heard that in a far-off country called Singapore a cat now exists who is extremely small in size, smaller than any other known breed. This has come about – mind you, I am only repeating travellers' tales – because everybody in that country is meant to work with the utmost diligence and produce useful and sought-after objects to swell the Gross National Product. As you are well aware, cats do not produce much in a material sense, except other cats, so we are not too highly esteemed there. In fact we are regarded as mere aesthetic objects or parasites – implying that we don't earn our keep.'

He paused for this unkind innuendo to be recognised as the pathetic fallacy it was.

'These Singapore cats – the males weigh barely half as much as you and I – grow up in the drains and spend most of their lives there, drains being comparatively safe places, rarely visited by politicians. Consequently the newly evolved breed is known as the Drain Cat.'

Drains! Sunshine felt sick to his stomach. He was thankful that nobody considered him an aesthetic object.

'It's possible there's some connection with the Brain Drain that Mr and Mrs speak of,' Kuching concluded.

Eden

I T WAS UNSEASONABLY sunny, quite paradisal weather, and a light lunch had been served in the garden. Sunshine was entertaining Sirikit – they were exchanging concepts – so Kuching went for a short walk on his own, partly out of tact and partly because the young lady's jejune pedagogics made him feel considerably more than his age. He didn't want to feature as a dog in the manger or a snake in the grass.

He passed the time of day with several acquaintances, and skilfully evaded the whizz-cat Ms Chatto with her inopportune designs on either his person or his past, he wasn't sure which. There was rather too much traffic about for his liking, and his old bones were a mite weary. (Humans seemed to be getting younger every day.) So before long he turned homewards.

A bowl of food had been upset, he noticed, and its contents scattered. But it wasn't his; he had emptied his before leaving. The two young cats were slightly ruffled, and also somewhat shamefaced, and began simultaneously to explain what had happened during his absence: it was a drunken pigeon, according to Sirikit; a thunderbolt, according to Sunshine.

Kuching permitted himself a faint smile. Turning to Sirikit, he said, 'Straight from the Ram Brewery down the road, I imagine.' To Sunshine he said, gazing into the cloudless sky, 'A bolt from the blue, eh?' He continued urbanely: 'Speaking for myself, I don't care what you do as long as you don't frighten the humans.'

Revolution!

THERE HAD BEEN excited talk about Feline Rights and Affairs of State, and things were coming to the boil. Sunshine himself grew quite warm on the subject.

'We need a spokescat who will speak for cats,' he told Kuching. 'It is time we made ourselves felt.'

The question was: What would they be made to feel in return? 'Talk not of rights,' said Kuching in his most unctuous tones. 'Talk rather of luck . . . and of adroit contrivance.'

Sunshine felt disappointed in his friend; but perhaps it was decreed that the fire of youth should one day fade into ashes.

The moment had brought forth its leader, a cat of middling dimensions and large self-importance who called himself Polly-tix. Sunshine thought the name had a fine ring to it. Kuching merely observed that it was normally associated with a big, talkative and unappealing variety of bird.

Polly-tix had recently moved there from Westminster way. He had splendid ideas for improving the condition of cats by various means, including Withdrawal of Labour. Some of his intended constituents pointed out that they didn't labour anyway, and they were conservative in tendency. Polly-tix promised to conserve even more thoroughly. All they had to do was unite under him. He would serve as their advo-cat.

He was bossy, but leaders had to be. Sunshine admired his fervour, but didn't much like it when he appointed Sirikit as his A-gent. Why couldn't he have picked on some daring young tom for that exacting responsibility? (One duty was to collect a modest proportion of each member's food, to be kept aside against emergencies; no one knew where it was kept.) Polly-tix claimed that for public relations he needed someone who had been in the public eye, but Sunshine didn't approve of the way he eyed Sirikit.

Meetings were held in a corner of the school playing-field, deserted at the moment because of the holidays. Demands were voiced for bigger and better helpings of food, and stricter punctuality, which would require humans to carry alarm clocks set for mealtimes. Also for improvements in the weather: it had been raining far too much of late. And of course – which aroused considerable enthusiasm – for Enhanced Respect. A scrawny member of the party related how he had been called a 'moggy' and kicked by the milkman, just because he was snoozing near some empty milk bottles. Another had had his tail pulled by young louts. (He didn't mention that some children had run up and driven the louts away, and then heaped loving and respectful words on him, plus a portion of fish and chips.) A third insisted that humans should take their hats off when meeting cats on the street, and dogs made to curtsy or bow, depending on their gender. A fourth wanted to be addressed as Spots *Esquire* or else *Sir*. And a fifth, a middle-aged black, complained that her Mr and Mrs behaved in an unduly familiar manner and kept calling her *Which* or possibly *Witch*.

Sunshine, who attended the meetings faithfully, reported part of these proceedings to Kuching. Kuching only said, 'We live in an imperfect society. Nowhere will you find a You-topia.'

On the next occasion, Sunshine spoke a few solemn words about You-topia, and how they must strive resolutely to find where it was. His remarks were well received, and Polly-tix gave him a friendly pat on the shoulder: 'You will go far in this brave new world of ours!'

'I'm not sure *I* want to go anywhere,' Sirikit murmured. 'The Cedars is good enough for me.'

'But You-topia is something that, once you've found it, you can bring home with you,' Sunshine reassured her. He hoped he was right about that. Then perhaps Mr and Mrs could share it.

When they got down to deciding who should actually do what, there was less agreement. Polly-tix tried to form them into working parties, but as soon as he stopped talking they disappeared in different directions. This meant that Sirikit had to go round to their houses, informing them of the date of the following meeting and urging them to be present. Some were rude to her, even hinting that she harboured improper ambitions.

Cats were inveterate individualists, Kuching reiterated. They did not hunt in packs. They believed in private enterprise, not collective agitation. Sunshine thought of sirgallerheading: it would come under the heading of private enter-prize, he imagined.

Much to his surprise, Kuching turned up for the next meeting. Polly-tix was more vehement than ever. He had come a long way since demanding a pedestrian precinct for cats and a free issue of flea-repellent collars four times a year. It was no time for idle sentiment, he announced, they must all sharpen their claws, and be ever on their guard. . . . Suddenly he halted and flung out a paw at a smallish, whitish duck, who had settled on the edge of the gathering: 'Seize that animal – he's a police informer!' But nobody stirred a limb. It was only a child's pet who had strayed out of a nearby garden, an amiable, stupid creature who wouldn't understand a word of what was being said.

'Let him do his worst!' Polly-tix roared, and went on to speak of a coo-day-tar, of marching in force on Buckingham Palace, and installing himself there as the National Leader. Indeed, he was thinking of pro-claiming himself king – whereupon, no matter the cost to his modesty, he would have a Magnificat specially composed for the occasion.

Subsequently, he would appoint his faithful followers to key positions in the life of the country, if not the world.

At this point Kuching roused himself. 'Would you by any chance have Irish blood in your veins, Your Majesty?' he asked mildly.

Polly-tix admitted that he did, just a few drops, by some chance.

'Then you will be acquainted with the history of the King of the Cats.' Kuching took the liberty of reminding the company that the King of the Cats could well look like any ordinary fellow – 'I am not suggesting that our friend here is *conspicuously* ordinary' – with no visible marks of distinction. Hence the time-honoured practice was to cut off a tiny slice of his ear: then, should he be authentic and destined for the throne, he would reveal his true nature by speaking in the human language. Which naturally Polly-tix would need to, if he were to lead his subjects to higher things, and humans to lower ones. 'In Ireland, I gather,' Kuching added, 'the King was given to voicing truths that humans didn't care to hear.'

So it was imperative, before they went any further, to establish Polly-tix's royal credentials beyond a shadow of a doubt by removing a piece of his ear. . . . Sleepers awoke; a hum of anticipation ran through the assembly. Something was happening at last.

'It won't hurt – not very much. You have sharp teeth, don't you, Sunshine?'

The self-appointed king, whose tail had been twitching uneasily for some time, shrank to half his former size. He mewled in terror, wriggled swiftly through a gap in the fence, and fled. He was never to be seen, or heard, in those parts again. So that was the end of Polly-tix.

'He's quite a guy, your friend,' Sirikit told Sunshine. 'That's the second time he's saved my bacon.'

Later, when congratulated on his resourcefulness, Kuching simply replied, 'A wise old feline called Hodge once said: "So far is it from being true that cats are naturally equal, that no two of them can be half an hour together without one acquiring an evident superiority over the other."'

A Good Deed In A Naughty World

T HERE WERE TWO old humans, man and wife, living some way off, in what Kuching described as a 'less desirable area'. They were too poor to feed their family – one old cat, one old dog – and themselves as well, so they themselves went short.

'A sorry story,' Kuching said. 'It shouldn't happen to a dog.' At one time, he told Sunshine, humans used to expose their old people on remote hillsides, where they eventually died of hunger or cold. These days they gave them a pen-shun instead, but the result could be much the same.

Was there some way of relieving the worthy old couple? Sirikit said she would gladly have given them a share of her tee-vee fee if she had ever seen it. Yorker proposed something he termed a 'Benefit Game', but this was dismissed out of hand. The Old Labrador suggested removing a joint of meat from the butcher's once a week and taking it to the old couple; but that dodge was well-worn, and in any case the Old Labrador was too slow to bring it off, as well as too honest.

There was money lying around in their house, Sunshine mentioned; he assumed the bits of coloured paper were money for they couldn't be worth keeping otherwise.

'That would be robbing Peter to pay Paul,' Kuching declared. 'And we have to remember that Peter is our Mr.' Charity ought to begin at home, and not stray too far afield.

An answer emerged when Sunshine spotted a leather object lying on the pavement, partly concealed under a privet hedge. He guessed it was a wallet, for he had seen Mr putting banknotes into a similar article. The chances were, there was money in this one, and it was quite fat.

'Send for the Old Labrador!' Kuching ordered. 'Quickly, before some dishonest person comes along and makes off with it!'

The Old Labrador soon lumbered up. 'Child's play!' he puffed, seizing on the wallet.

Kuching instructed him to go up to the door of the old couple's little house and push the wallet through the letter-box. 'But don't ring the bell!'

The Old Labrador found no difficulty in opening the slot of the letter-box with a paw and pushing the wallet through. It fell with a satisfying thud.

'Well done!' Kuching exclaimed. 'Now let's fade modestly away.'

The old man had heard the noise and came slowly to the door, but all he saw was a dog disappearing round the corner, together with two cats. They seemed to be good friends, like his own cat and dog. It was a cheering sight.

Unfortunately the old couple were as honest as they were poor, and they took the wallet to the police station at once. When the policeman opened it, it was seen to be crammed with credit cards, membership cards, railway passes, addresses and telephone numbers, photographs, and licences to do this and that.

Fortunately the owner was so delighted when he came to collect his property, all of it intact, that he insisted on giving the reluctant old couple a handsome reward of ten pounds.

The Bottom Of The Mind

S IRIKIT WAS MUCH concerned for her brother. He had been behaving strangely, or not at all. He had completely lost interest in ladies, which wasn't good for his career, although his wife seemed happy about it.

'He had to go to a special vet,' Sirikit divulged, 'a sigh-cat-trist who knows about the inside of the head. The sigh-cat-trist believes that my brother is in love with his mother.'

'Is he?' This came as a revelation to Sunshine; hitherto he had thought only of mothers loving their children.

'He says he doesn't know.'

'What does his mother say?'

'She died years ago.'

The psychiatrist was convinced there were dark elements lurking at the bottom of Prem's mind, all sorts of things he had forgotten about, and they had to be brought to the surface. He described some of them, and they were very rude. Prem told him that in that case he didn't wish to remember them, thank you.

'The sigh-cat-trist kept saying they would have to dig deeper – you'd think Prem was a potato patch. One day he was reciting a long list of the things Prem unconsciously wanted to do – Prem hadn't heard of most of them, they were in a foreign language – and Prem said there was one thing he consciously wanted to do. And he did it.'

'What was it he did? But perhaps you'd rather not –'

'He went for the man and clawed him and pummelled him so badly that he had to go to hospital. Now he refuses to see Prem any more.'

'Oh dear – but how is Prem?'

'He insists he's completely cured. And he's beginning to – to look at females again; it's all one to him whether they're thoroughbred or not – *free association* is how he puts it. His Mr and Mrs are very pleased, they think the treatment was worth the expense. For some reason they've renamed him Eedipuss, but he doesn't mind, because Eedipuss was an illustrious king.'

Dissident

P ERCHED ON AN armchair, Kuching announced 'a tale of our times'. Sunshine was lying under the chair. He cocked his ears.

It took place in one of those unfortunate countries in the eastern parts of Europe. A senior British politician had given the dictator of this country a sweet little puppy: 'a cheap way of making friends, I would say.' (Kuching refrained from indicating that the puppy was a Labrador.) The dictator took this as a tribute to his firm and unswerving rule. He was so proud that he had the puppy borne through the streets of the capital in a triumphal procession of motor cars and bodyguards, while the people took off their hats, if they had any. Ordinary citizens went hungry, but the puppy was fed on the finest meat, while dog biscuits were sent from Britain ('famous for such things') to supplement its diet. It wanted for nothing.

Whenever the puppy ('who had a name sounding like *Chowcheskew*') felt unwell, generally through overeating, it was taken to the best hospital in the land. On one occasion a cat – described later as a *dissident* ('this means one who sits by himself') – attacked the puppy there, though without inflicting mortal injuries. The secret police as well as the not so secret were called in at once, along with their most up-to-date weaponry, imported from abroad like the biscuits, and they searched high and low, upsetting the beds, knocking down the doctors and nurses, and breaking other objects in their zeal, but they couldn't find the cat. In his rage the dictator ordered the hospital to be blown up. 'Which was rather a pity.'

'What about the brave cat?'

'At liberty to this day, as far as we know. Naturally a lot of other cats, perfectly innocent ones, came to a sticky end.'

Kittens' College

SOMETHING LINGERED ON of those communal aspirations and the notion of self-help, and there had been talk of setting up an Acatemy for the education of the young. Eventually the elders decided to go ahead, using a deserted shack on the edge of some waste land; it smelt of ghostly, long-departed mice, but no one minded that.

Matronly cats made pronouncements about 'the alarming ignorance of today's youth' and 'filling a pressing need'. But when the school opened, the kittens fought or played (often with their would-be teachers' tails) instead of attending to lessons. And then the parents started to find fault with what was being taught: useless subjects, they claimed, like mewing in unison, pussyfooting, and painting free-style paw-traits. Moreover, it was a bore, having to take the kittens to school and then come to collect them, since, as they put it, 'We might be busy sleeping at the time.' This problem was solved when the Old Labrador offered to call and wake them up.

Making objections, it seemed, was a feline characteristic. A proposal that Sirikit should teach Personal Hygiene was ill received: the parents asked, did she suppose the children came from dirty homes? Sunshine thought of offering classes on Love And What It Means To Us, but feared it would be deemed indelicate. Kuching was invited to give a course of lectures on Famous Cats In History – all concerned approved of this, except the kittens, and they weren't consulted – but declined on the grounds that he didn't much care to talk about himself.

So, what with disagreement over the syllabus plus the natural inclinations of the pupils, most of the time in the Acatemy was Playtime, although the organisers liked to believe that it included such instructive exercises as Cat-and-Mouse, Self-Defence and Pre-emptive Attack, The Art of Telling Tails, Sardines, Dog's Breakfast, and Improving Your Purrsonality.

Enthusiasm quickly waned; except among the kittens, in whom it waxed. The Acatemy closed abruptly when several rough-looking humans staggered into the premises one day, carrying bottles and blankets (far more malodorous than the mice), and making uncouth noises. Cats and kittens left at once.

Clever Clogs

'**Y**OU HAVE SEVERAL times asked me to tell you about Famous Cats,' Kuching informed Sunshine and Sirikit. 'Since I am feeling wide awake this afternoon, I shall tell you of just one of them.'

This is what he told them.

Once upon a time there was a miller who had fallen on hard times ('never mind what a miller is, Sunshine, it doesn't matter'), largely because of cheap foreign imports. When he died of chagrin, as he did, he had nothing to leave his sons but one mill, one ass ('no, Sunshine, the ass is a lowly hard-working relative of the Noble Horse') and one cat, whose job it had been to chase mice out of the granary. The eldest son received the mill, the second the ass, and the third the cat, who will henceforward simply be called Puss.

The youngest son was very miserable. 'My two brothers can join together and earn a livelihood of sorts,' he said aloud, 'but once I have eaten the cat' ('pull yourself together, Sunshine!') 'and made a pair of mittens out of the fur, I shall be left with nothing' ('mittens, Sirikit, not kittens: you put them on your paws').

At this, Puss spoke up ('he can be forgiven for breaking the golden rule'): 'Do not distress yourself unduly. Just provide me with a stout pair of boots for my hind feet so that I can venture into the brambles, and also a stout bag, and you will find that you are not so badly off as you imagined.'

The son worked for a cobbler for a whole month and was rewarded with a strong pair of boots made of leather, just the right size for Puss, and a bag with a string to close it tight.

Puss placed some lettuce and bran in the bag, and settled down quietly by a rabbit warren. Before long a young rabbit, uninstructed in the ways of the world, came out and crawled into the bag, whereupon Puss tightened the string round the bag and dispatched him.

Puss went to the King's palace and asked to see His Majesty. He made a profound bow, and informed the King that his master, the Count of Catabas (a grand name he made up), had sent a small gift as a token of his loyalty and respect. The King, who was fond of rabbit stew, was very pleased.

The next day Puss hid in a cornfield, with his bag open, and trapped a brace of partridges ('or else a couple'), and took them to the King. The King was very pleased again, and gave Puss a *pooer-bwah* ('an upper-class expression meaning "for-drink", a pint of milk, no doubt, or a small pot of cream').

Over the following weeks Puss returned to the palace bearing other small edible items, caught (he said) by his master, the Count, an accomplished hunter.

He learnt that on a particular day the King would be driving with his beautiful young daughter along the bank of a nearby river. So he said to his master ('the word has inverted commas round it, of course'): 'If you follow my instructions to the letter you will make your fortune. What I want you to do is strip naked and bathe in the river, and leave the rest to me. But for heaven's sake hide those disgraceful old clothes of yours!'

'Aren't you getting too big for your boots?' asked the bewildered young man. 'No, they are a perfect fit, thank you.' Puss watched with satisfaction as the youth flapped about in the water, turning blue with cold; he hadn't forgotten the threat to eat him and make mittens out of his fur.

When the royal entourage arrived at the spot, Puss began to jump about and shout, 'Help, help! The Count is drowning!' The King's guards dived into the water and pulled the young man out, while Puss, whom the King greeted warmly, explained that thieves had stolen the Count's clothes while he was bathing.

The King ordered the Count to be dressed in the finest garments in the royal wardrobe, which accompanied him wherever he went. This was done. The Princess peeped at the young man from under modestly lowered eyelids, and the young man, once he was dry and warm, cast fond glances at the Princess. The two of them entered the coach with the King, who wished to continue the drive.

Puss, however, ran on ahead, until he came to a fine large meadow, full of plump sheep with thick glossy fleeces. He approached the shepherds, and said sternly: 'Now, my men, you will tell the King that this meadow and everything in it belongs to the Count of Catabas – or else you will be chopped up and made into hamburgers.' They were so terrified that, when the King drove up and asked who owned the meadow, they answered accordingly.

Puss hastened further, and came to a big factory where cars were made. He went up to the workers and directed them to tell the King that the factory was the sole property of the Count of Catabas: if they didn't, they would all be consigned to the crusher. They promised to do as he ordered.

Puss hurried onwards, and arrived at a magnificent castle belonging to a wealthy Ogre ('a giant with bad habits'), who in fact owned all the land around, the sheep in the meadow, and the factory as well.

Puss rang the bell, and said that he happened to be passing and could not refrain from paying his respects. The Ogre was a fearful ty-rant ('which means he was always shouting'), but he responded as civilly as his sort can, which is not very, and Puss proceeded thus: 'I have heard, though it is hard to credit, that you have the power to change yourself into any shape you wish, such as an elephant or a tiger.' To prove this was true, the Ogre turned himself into a tiger, snarling so fiercely that Puss was alarmed ('I bet!' gasped Sirikit) and clawed his way up a tree growing in the courtyard. This was difficult to do because of the boots he was wearing ('but, as you know, fear lends wings').

Having slid to the ground again, Puss said: 'That's all very well, sir, but I cannot believe you have the power to turn yourself into something very small – like a mouse, say. That would be utterly impossible!'

'O thou of little faith!' cried the Ogre. 'Just you watch me!' And he changed into a mouse, which Puss promptly pounced on and swallowed up. ('Hurrah!')

Just then the royal party reached the castle, and they marvelled at the towers and battlements. Puss welcomed them in, explaining that the castle belonged to the Count of Catabas. The King was amazed. 'What a tiptop establishment! And it belongs to you, my dear young Count, with all the land around – not to mention the car plant, which I notice is equipped with the latest technology! I can hardly believe my eyes!'

But he did believe them, for waiting inside was a sumptuous banquet, long tables laden with all the food and drink that kings are fond of. Actually the Ogre had prepared the feast for his friends, but they had spotted the King and his guards and thought it wise to slink home.

After the King had taken seven or eight glasses of superb vintage wine, he declared that the only thing left to wish for was that the Count would marry his daughter, the Princess. The two young people expressed their readiness to oblige on the spot, and they all lived happily ever after.

Especially Puss, who put his boots away since the castle was fitted with wall-to-wall carpeting, and thereafter wore them only on special occasions.

We can assume that the Princess had really fallen in love with Puss, but saw that if she wanted to live with him she would have to marry the Count. As for Puss, he became a Fine Gentlecat – not a king, which is too troublesome – and no longer chased after mice except when he felt in need of diversion or exercise. That was only fair – which is why this is called a fairy tale.

'And there you have a Famous Cat in History,' Kuching concluded, quite exhausted by his eloquence. 'Typically kind-hearted, unselfish, brave, and exceedingly smart.'

'Ah,' murmured Sunshine wisely.

'I bet he was a first-class cricketer,' offered Yorker, who had joined them towards the end of the story and hadn't taken much of it in, 'before he hung his boots up.'

'I think it's a lovely story,' Sirikit trilled, 'except for the bit about the horrid tiger. And Puss – wasn't he smashing! I'd have married him in a flash if I'd had the chance.'

'Oh,' mumbled Sunshine glumly.

'I mean, if I were living in a fairy tale.'

Second Course

K UCHING HAD HARDLY stirred over the past few days. Could it be cat-alepsy, Sunshine wondered. He tried to coax him into the garden. 'Your scent needs freshening,' he hinted, for without it the garden wasn't half so satisfying, but Kuching only murmured cryptically about ab-scents making the heart grow fonder.

'Are you off your food?'

'Cats want but little here below, nor want that little long,' said Kuching. 'Though it has to be of the finest quality.'

He looked pensive, or would have done had he not been yawning broadly.

Of late, he intimated, he had been thinking a lot about the wise old Persian, though he couldn't imagine why. Unless perhaps that, towards the end, one recalled the beginnings. But this theory he kept to himself.

'He was my guide and mentor, and but for him my youth would have been ill spent. As Persians are prone to, he would sit for hours, preferably in front of the fire, "meditating on the problems of metaphysics", in the apt words of a human scribe, one Somerset Morning. The things he knew! And, as an inevitable consequence, I too know. . . . When he was himself young, he told me, he would eagerly frequent Doctors and Saints, and heard much argument.'

'Mr and Mrs were having an argument last night,' Sunshine put in. 'About whether they should watch one programme on tee-vee or another.'

'Not the same kind of argument at all. He was a great philosopher, a true sophisti-cat. Of stately appearance, and a kindly and equable tempera-ment, unlike many of his race, who incline to long hairs and short tempers.'

He nodded off for five minutes. Sunshine sat very still and waited.

'Sleep,' said Kuching, with another large yawn, 'I always say, is great Nature's second course. . . . But what were we discussing? Ah yes, the old

Persian. I remember a pleasing story of his, about their celebrated prophet, Muhammad, and how one day he was called away while his highly respected cat was sleeping on the sleeve of his robe, and the Prophet cut off the sleeve so as not to disturb the cat. . . . The old Persian was much courted by humans, they could divine his superior nature, and they loved his company. He used to say that when he played with his humans, who could tell whether he wasn't entertaining them more than they entertained him?'

That *was* a peculiar and clever thought. Sunshine pondered. There might well be some important truth in it somewhere. One day he too would be able to mention a wise old cat who had told him this and taught him that. But not yet.

'By the way,' Kuching said in a changed tone of voice. 'I've been making discreet enquiries, and it seems that your mother was a respectable young lady who fell in love with a handsome adventurer – your father, in other words – and ran away with him. Sad to say, he disappeared before long, presumably on another adventure. She succumbed to a broken heart directly after you came into the world, having first expressed her undying love for her one and only offspring. You were adopted by a humble couple of kittenless cats, but they were advanced in years, and . . .'

Kuching had made all this up. It *could* be true. There was no one to confirm it, or to deny it.

Sunshine didn't know what to say. It would take time for these revelations to sink in. So he said, 'Oh. . . . Thank you.'

Kuching closed his eyes again. He felt like a second helping of Nature's second course.

Happy Lands

SIRIKIT WAS MOST sympathetic when Sunshine confided his anxieties, for she wasn't flighty all through. If she had been, she would have flown before now.

'He *is* getting on a bit,' she said. 'So's everybody else, more or less. Even a poor snail, when a human squashes him, suffers as much as when a cat is trodden on. Or so I've heard, though it sounds unlikely.'

They were silent for a while.

'He's been good to both of us,' she resumed. 'Where I come from – where my people came from – they would say that he must have stored up lots and lots of merits.'

Sunshine recollected how the bowl-bearing Old Labrador had rambled on about merits. 'They're good for you, aren't they?'

'They're supposed to help us get to a marvellous land where there are *nimfs* waiting – elegant young males, and lovely young females too, I expect – and the sun shines all the time, and nobody hungers or thirsts any more. There's a river that flows with milk and honey – I don't know what honey is, but it must be something delicious.'

'Yum-yum!' A fine spot to spend one's retirement, Sunshine fancied. 'Whereabouts is it?'

'Too far to walk, that's for sure! You can only go there after you've stopped walking – after you've stopped doing everything. That's the rule.'

'You don't mean. . . ?'

'Yes, I do. But you don't stay there very long, because if you did, you'd get used to it and grow bored.'

He found that hard to believe.

'You see, there's a still better place, more refined, where there isn't anything at all – there's just nothing.'

'But wouldn't that be dreadfully boring?' Nothing didn't seem much to look forward to.

'They say no, it's not, because there's nothing there to bore you. And by then you don't *want* anything, so you're never discontented.'

The two agreed that it was all a great mystery, and you just had to Wait and See.

'And we'll just have to wait and see what the vet says,' Sunshine added. 'It's probably only some little indisposition – like cat-arrh or lass-itude . . .'

Sirikit promised to keep her toes crossed.

Something, Sometime

K UCHING HAD GONE to see the vet, someone he had grown almost fond of. Sunshine waited at home, nervously, where Sirikit joined him. (Kuching had grown fond of her too. She could wind Sunshine round her little claw, he reflected, but still, the lad was in pretty good hands, so to speak.) At one point the Old Labrador peered in at the gate and nodded to them. 'Ah,' he mumbled, 'hm', and wobbled sadly off.

When Kuching returned, he was rather quiet; at such times the stoutest of cats will need a little restorative lie-down. Sunshine went on waiting, washing his paws a touch too assiduously. Sirikit scampered some way up the trunk of a small tree, then came down, looking faintly flustered.

Finally Kuching said mildly, 'As I expected, it's the kidneys.'

'Oh?' whispered Sunshine.

'Well, it has to be *something*,' Kuching said reasonably, '*sometime*, doesn't it?'

'Ah?'

'They're giving me injections and the like. It's nothing out of the ordinary. Part of Nature. Or even, you could say, Life. We cats, being sensible creatures on the whole, don't think too deeply when thinking is of no avail. . . . Mrs held my paw while the vet was about his business – and, you know, I actually found it comforting, like a –' Like a mother, he would have said, but he didn't want to set his young friend off.

'Like a mother!' Sirikit burst out.

'Does it hurt?' Sunshine managed to say. Sirikit looked the other way. An ambulance was heard clamouring not far off; Sunshine hoped it wouldn't stop outside their gate.

Kuching, who appeared to have dozed off, roused himself.

'Not at all unbearably. Medicine, it must be admitted, has made considerable advances since I was a kitten with the colic. . . . There's some

133

difficulty in – in passing water, to use an expression I picked up in the surgery. It goes in easily, but it doesn't always come out easily.'

Sunshine felt very sorrowful, and showed it. Sirikit surreptitiously shook a tear away. Perhaps it should be mentioned that she would soon – we can make the joke safely since she isn't listening – she would soon be having Sirikittens. Female cats are often in this condition, so no one commented on it; and neither shall we.

'I've advised you before not to show your feelings too plainly, Sunshine. It's not considered *comme il faut* in polite society, as the young lady will confirm. Oh do cheer up! I'm not ready yet for my requies-cat. Or for an Elegy by Cat-ullus. . . . That poem you made about Mr and Mrs – oh yes, I know, I know, very little escapes me – actually it wasn't too bad, as poetry goes.'

Sunshine swelled up with quiet pride.

'Mind you, I trust you won't make a habit of it. . . . In point of fact I too am capable of turning the occasional couplet. I shall recite an example:

> Fate now the forfeit of eight lives retains,
> And e'en the ninth creeps languid through my veins.

A couplet has much to recommend it; it doesn't go on and on . . .'

Kuching paused to admire his couplet, or possibly the practical advantages of the verse form in question.

'No, I'm not finished with you yet. There's still time for me to pass on a little more worldly wisdom.'

'Please do!' Sunshine chirruped joyfully. His friend might tease him, but surely he would never fib to him.

THE SUN SLANTED in through the tall windows. Kuching basked in it contentedly. The sun moved across the carpet little by little. Wherever it was, Kuching was in it. Here, then there, then a little further away. Until eventually, as it sank, the sun began to crawl feebly up the far wall, across the foot of the bookshelves, and faded away.

The funny thing was, wherever the sun lay, there lay Kuching, apparently fast asleep, and no one saw him get up and move. It was as if the sun bore him gently, imperceptibly, with it.